Iza Duffus Hardy

**Love in Idleness**

The story of a winter in Florida. Vol. 1

Iza Duffus Hardy

**Love in Idleness**
*The story of a winter in Florida. Vol. 1*

ISBN/EAN: 9783337257132

Printed in Europe, USA, Canada, Australia, Japan

Cover: Foto ©Andreas Hilbeck / pixelio.de

More available books at **www.hansebooks.com**

# THE STORY OF A WINTER IN FLORIDA

BY

## IZA DUFFUS HARDY

AUTHOR OF 'HEARTS OR DIAMONDS?' 'THE LOVE THA
'ORANGES AND ALLIGATORS' ETC.

'Yet marked I where the bolt of Cupid fell :
It fell upon a little western flower,—
Before milk-white, now purple with Love's
And maidens call it Love-in-Idleness!'
*A Midsumme*

IN THREE VOLUMES

## VOL. I.

London

## F. V. WHITE & CO.

31 SOUTHAMPTON STREET, ST

1387

# CONTENTS

OF

# THE FIRST VOLUME.

———◆◇◆———

# LOVE IN IDLENESS.

## CHAPTER I.

### THE ATLANTIC COAST EXPRESS.

THE prospect of a journey of over a thousand miles, to be taken alone, was not in the least degree alarming to Violet Preston; nor need it be, indeed, to even the most timorous of English girls, when the thousand miles are to be passed in an American Pullman car. Violet Preston was an English girl, and in some things she was timorous; she was apt to scream at a rat and run away from a black-beetle; but she would have undertaken the week's railway journey, from the Atlantic to

the Pacific coast, by herself, with the utmost
equanimity, and would have set off on a voyage
round the world far more serenely than she
would have faced a large cockroach. Still,
while the *rôle* of the solitary and indepen-
dent traveller had no terrors, and even possessed a certain charm, for her, she was not
sorry to find that, although she was alone in
the sense of not being under the protection of
any members of her family nor attached to any
party of friends, yet she would not be altogether without escort, as Max Randolph happened to be going by the same southward-bound
train that bore her from New York to Florida.

The Pullman 'buffet sleeping-car' was
crowded from front to rear, each 'section'
packed with its pile of small hand-baggage. It
was only early December, too early for the
real rush to Florida to have commenced; but
it was apparent from the aspect of the car

that the tide of northern travel had already well begun to set southwards.   It was evening; the lamps were lit and the windows closed; there was quite a cheerful, cosy, home-like look about the interior of the car, which held out ample promise of comfort for the Florida-bound passengers, to whom this car was to be dining, sleeping, dressing, and drawing-room for the next two days.

'Time's up!' observed the conductor smilingly, as a delicate hint to the ladies who were embracing and bidding each other goodbye. 'Come! hurry up!' he added more familiarly to a knot of young men, who were hilariously wringing each other's hands, and slapping each other on the back, and blocking up the narrow gangway.

Mr. Randolph had no farewells to make, except so far as he took a light and friendly share in Miss Preston's.  She had a grandfather and a cousin come to see her off; she was fond of them both, but it was with smiles and not with tears that she was parting from them.

'There's somebody has the upper berth in your section, my dear child,' observed her grandfather disapprovingly, looking at a heap of hand-baggage on the seat opposite to hers.

(For the benefit of those of my readers who have not enjoyed the pleasure of a journey in an American Pullman 'sleeper,' let me explain that, of the two seats which compose each 'section,' the one facing the engine commands the lower berth, whilst the passenger who is seated back to the engine mounts to the upper berth.)

'I wish we had booked a whole section for Violet,' continued her grandfather; 'is it too late to make a change?'

'Never mind, grandpapa,' Miss Preston said

cheerfully; 'I dare say it's some other girl, who may be a pleasant companion.'

'It looks like a man's valise,' observed her cousin Tom, throwing cold water on this comfortable suggestion.

'Come, time's up, father,' he added, in obedience to the conductor's repeated intimation. 'You will be all right, Violet. I dare say Randolph will see to your baggage and all that.'

'Yes, I'll look after Miss Violet well,' Mr. Randolph assured them. Then there was a confusion of hurried handshakings and kissings and parting messages.

'Love to Granny.' 'Love to Rosemary.' 'Write soon!' 'Goodbye!' and Violet Preston's relatives, and various other passengers' relatives and friends, took their departure.

The Englishmen descended from the car just in time, before the train began to move;

the Americans of course waited until it was fairly in motion, and then some of them lingered still until the very last moment that it was safe, before they swung themselves from the steps of the moving cars.

Violet Preston's heart was light, and her face radiant with smiles, as she waved her hand in farewell to her friends.

She was on her way to Florida, to spend the winter with her dearest friend, Rosemary Heath, whom she loved as a sister, and another friend was by happy chance her escort. Mr. Randolph and she were too frankly good friends and comrades for her even to endeavour to disguise, either from herself or from him, that it *was* a happy chance, to her mind; and with the utmost simplicity and straightforwardness she had expressed herself as 'so glad' to find that he too was going South that very evening.

She settled herself contentedly into her seat

amongst her various packages. Although she had travelled a great deal, she had never attained to the accomplishment of reducing her *impedimenta* to a minimum. Violet Preston was exceedingly feminine in many things; and in her lack of the faculty of condensing and compressing all her small necessaries into one receptacle she was the veriest woman—although she envied those strong sisters who travel with one valise, as happy man can so easily do. Miss Preston had a collection of bags in assorted sizes, a luncheon basket, and a bundle. Amongst this array of her minor baggage she sat in state, and looked up at Mr. Randolph with the sisterly smile she usually kept ready for him. Max Randolph, standing leaning his hand on the back of the seat, smiled responsively down on her. If there were just the faintest touch of a little new shyness in her smile, a shade of greater distance and deference than usual in

his free and easy air, it was only the most in-
finitesimal shade, due to the new circumstances
in which this young man and woman found
themselves thrown together.

'And where is your section?' inquired
Violet.

'Right at the other end of the car, but well
within call,' he added reassuringly.

'I wonder who my fellow-traveller is,' she
said, looking at the valise on the opposite
seat.

'Not the fat man, it is to be hoped,' he
replied, casting an indicative glance in the
direction of a gentleman of fine aldermanic
proportions; 'he'd fill up the whole section!'

'Horrible thought!' said Violet. 'If it *is*
he, my only hope is that he may spend his time
in the smoking-car. There certainly isn't room
for him and his portmanteau here. There's
room for *you*,' she added, with another sisterly

smile, drawing her basket to one side, as the engineer was now putting on steam, and the oscillation of the car made it awkward for those who were essaying to stand with steadfast footing and graceful preservation of equilibrium.

Mr. Randolph sat down with alacrity.

'So we are really off to Florida!' he observed.

'To Florida—and Rosemary.'

'Oh yes; Miss Rosemary of course is the more important objective point. How does she like Florida life?'

'Not very much, I fancy. She finds it lonely. It is a very secluded life—very dull for *her*.'

' Doesn't like wasting her sweetness on the desert air, eh ? '

' Her own people have settled in a very lonely part. But, you know,' Miss Preston continued in narrative tone, 'we, Rose and I, are going to stay at her uncle's place, West Grove House, and when we get there, I think she will enjoy herself much more. For one thing—such is feminine vanity—I think that my being with her will make a little difference.'

'Not impossible. I've heard of stranger things.'

'And what will make even more difference,' Violet added, with a quiet smile, 'is that the uncle has got about twenty young men boarding there.'

'Miss Rosemary will be in her element, then,' he said. 'Twenty? You'll have a good time, won't you? Ten apiece.'

'Why don't you join the party?' she inquired. 'I dare say Mr. Whitworth could take you in.'

'Tail end of a *queue* of twenty?' he rejoined. 'No, thanks!'

'Why "*tail* end"?' she laughed. 'Why not *head*?'

'Why, certainly,' he agreed promptly; 'head's my place, isn't it?' and he softly hummed the opening bars of 'See the Conquering Hero comes!' under his breath.

'That's the air for you!' said Violet, laughing the pretty low laugh which was one of her charms.

'You always set me in my rightful place,' he replied with a lazy sort of half-smile—as if it was too much trouble to make it a whole one.

He was leaning back in his seat with his usual air of careless nonchalance, and glanced up from under his brows with a quietly humorous under-glance that was as common to him.

His secretive eyes—eyes which told no story, yet not for the want of any tale to tell! —always seemed to hold 'hidden springs of

mirth' in their depths. Sometimes the laugh
that lurked there was almost a sneer; but, as a
general thing, the somewhat ironic humour in
Max Randolph's eyes hurt nobody, for it was
quite as likely to be at his own expense as at
anyone else's.

His superficial attitude was indolent and indifferent; he walked through the world with a
chronic air of not seeing anything on his way
that was worth exciting himself about. This
crust of imperturbability broke up now and
then—though not many people had seen it
break up; and of the very few who had, Violet
Preston was not one.

Mr. Randolph was passably good-looking,
though his best friends had never been heard
to call him handsome. His face was rather
long and rather thin, the cheeks slightly hol-
lowed, the general cast of his features of a dis-
tinctively American type; and the intonation of

his voice also revealed his nationality, although it had no faintest touch of what we know as the 'Yankee twang'; it was rather the soft *trainante* accent of the South. He was tall, long-limbed, of rather slight than stalwart build, yet not lacking in strength, though the strength was probably more nervous than muscular. His dead brown hair, straight as an Indian's, grew low on his forehead; he had a heavy brown moustache, and long, sleepy, almond-shaped grey eyes, that did not often open quite wide under their level brows.

Violet Preston's personal appearance ranked far higher up in the scale of attraction than did his. If he was not handsome, even in the report of his friends, few even of her rivals questioned *her* right and title to beauty, though of course there were those—chiefly women—who 'did not admire her style.' Although she was, as I have said, an English girl, she came of

Irish race on her mother's side ; and the traces
of her Irish mother's blood were clear in Violet's
lovely face, especially in the colouring, in the
contrast of her dark hair and lashes with her
deep blue eyes and exquisitely fair skin, fine as
a rose-leaf.

Max Randolph, an artist, and with an
artist's eye, admired her, but never waxed enthusiastic about her charms. *She* thought *him*
' not handsome, but nice—very nice.' Violet,
like most of her sisters and countrywomen,
would have found it very difficult to get on
without that adaptive and universally serviceable adjective—' nice ! '

On the whole, these two friends estimated
the degree and quality of each other's attractions very fairly, neither overvaluing nor de-
preciating their respective qualities.

They had not sat chatting many minutes
when the other occupant of the section ap-

peared upon the scene, with a deprecatory bow, and a polite 'Excuse me, Madam!' He was fortunately not the fat man; he was long and lean and lanthorn-jawed; and albeit his voice was low, his pure nasal accent was strong to smite the ear.

Mr. Randolph eyed him without ill-will, but with an air of impartially and judicially deciding that he wished him somewhere else, as the new-comer began turning over his portable property, and to facilitate his movements Max vacated his seat, but still stood close by.

Presently, further down the car, a child was heard to set up a pitiful cry for 'bed,' and the negro porter, tall and young and coal-black, in a white calico jacket that made him look blacker, began to pull down one of the 'berths' that shut up so neatly into the ceiling, and to haul out curtains and mattresses. Violet cast a casual glance in that direction, and Max

Randolph, promptly following her eye, needed no other hint, but observed that it was about time for him to betake himself to his own camp, wished her a friendly good-night, and sauntered away down the car.

The other occupant of the section also discreetly betook himself off; and Miss Preston, having attracted the attention of the 'proud young porter,' and intimated to him that she desired to have her berth made up, went forth to grapple with the toilette difficulty—which is the one and only drawback of Pullman-car travelling.

Violet Preston, however, was sufficiently accustomed to nights on the cars to surmount the difficulty gracefully. She had provided herself with a dainty little pink embroidered jacket, in which she looked as pretty as a picture and as fresh as a rose, when she returned from the 'Ladies' Toilette Room,' which title dignifies a cupboard in which you could not swing the tiniest kitten. The curtains all along the car were bulging and waving into eccentric curves, mutely eloquent of the struggles with the toilette problem going on behind their folds, as Violet made her way back along the narrow passage between the rows of beds ; and she had not been snugly ensconced in the curtained recess of her berth many minutes when a mighty scrambling and shuffling testified that the stranger who was allotted as her *compagnon de voyage* was mounting into the berth above her ; his ascent being additionally evidenced by the ocular demonstration of a pair of feet in huge crimson woollen socks dangling for a moment before the narrow opening in the curtains before being drawn up to their destination.

Night and silence fell on the sleeping-car— silence only broken by the grampus-like snorts

and snores of a deeply slumbering traveller—
for as 'every bean hath its black,' and every
rose its thorn, so every Pullman car has its
snorer.

Violet pulled up the blind from her window
and looked out into the darkness. The sight
of the grey shadowy landscape, the dusky blots
and blurs of objects that were shapeless and
colourless in the obscurity, the black spectral
forms of the trees flying past, the distant lamps
glimmering faintly across dim fields—all had a
charm for her. She was in a mood to find a
charm in everything. She was fond of travelling;
she loved Rosemary; she was full of dreams of
the Sunny South. And she was on her way to
Fair Florida—to dear Rosemary, and with Max
Randolph to see her safely through the journey.
That was a part of the pleasure of the position
certainly. He would take good care of her,
she knew; and, although there was a streak of

independence in her nature, yet she felt it could not be otherwise than altogether pleasant to be taken care of by a friend and brother like Max Randolph.

When, later on in the night, she was awakened by a bang and a crash consequent on the uncoupling of the car from one train, and backing another train on to it more violently than was necessary, she closed her eyes again placidly. If there were anything wrong, Max Randolph would come and rouse her. In such an eminently desirable and peaceful frame of mind, lulled by the rock and rush of the train as it swept on its southward way, she sank back into the sweet sleep of youth, health, and hope.

## CHAPTER II.

### SOUTHWARD HO!

IN the morning Miss Preston awoke fresh and
happy. The toilette difficulty faced her again,
and she rose to meet it cheerfully. It is a
greater difficulty in the morning than over
night, as all the women-folk in the car, getting
ready for breakfast, make a rush to avail themselves of the severely limited toilette accommodation at much about the same time; and
Violet found the door of the dressing-room
besieged by several other ladies in more or less
dishevelled condition, variously armed with
divers articles of the toilette, one embracing a
comb and brush, another palpably secreting
beneath a shawl a toothbrush and sponge, while

from out of a small and bulging bag borne by a third—who wore a woollen scarf tied on as a hood—peeped what was evidently a beautifully curled and braided head of hair.

Violet, hustled and hurried, and amiably anxious to be obliging to her fellow-travellers, sought in vain an opportunity of seclusion for the brushing and plaiting of her long dark hair ; and finally, as the porter had officiously hastened to shut up her bed and take down her curtains, she was reduced to resign herself to the semi-publicity of the narrow slip of passage at the drawing-room end of the car. There Max Randolph, on his way from the smoking-car, stowing away a pipe in his pocket, came upon her suddenly, occupied, mermaid-like, with a comb and pocket-glass, with her hair all about her shoulders.

He had never known before how long and how thick was that silky dark hair !

Returning to her own section, she bade the porter put up the little table, ordered her coffee and eggs, and enjoyed a solitary little breakfast, as the fellow-occupant of the section, with delicate consideration for the probable feelings of a young lady travelling alone, took his morning meal with an acquaintance in another part of the car. Mr. Randolph also breakfasted in his own quarters, but immediately after breakfast came to make ample inquiries after Violet's comfort and cheer her—if she needed cheering—with a little social conversation.

They had crossed the wide, grey, gleaming waters of the Potomac, and had a view of the great white cupola of the Washington Capitol, rearing its snowy crown into the sky. Later on they had left the city of Richmond—the ex-capital of the Confederacy, teeming with memories of the Lost Cause—behind. Then

the rest of the day passed in speeding through
neutral-tinted fields—grey, brown, and drab,
the warmest bits of the landscape being where
here and there the winter woods retained
touches of their autumnal colouring, those
streaks of red-russet and yellow looking the
richer by contrast with the burnt patches,
black and bare, whereon the frequent forest-
fires had devoured the brushwood, and left the
skeleton trees standing where the 'merry green
woods' had been.

The passengers beguiled the time in the
usual ways. Most of the men who did not
play cards resorted to the smoking-car; the
women who were not reading paper-covered
novels did Berlin wool or crochet work; and
Max Randolph and Violet Preston talked.

Max talked of himself a good deal; he
always did; he liked the subject, and so did
she; and there was not much to say about the

landscape through which they were passing, although it set them off on a train of reminiscences of the gorgeous effects of the 'fall' colouring on the Hudson river in general, and of a certain picnic on its banks in particular. And dinner-time came and went, and the afternoon wore on, and the rain came down and splashed and pattered on the window-panes; outside, the sky was grey and the landscape looked desolate in the rain, and the only little gleanings of interest to be gathered from the outlook were when they passed through villages, and all the inhabitants, white and black, turned out to see the Florida express pass, just as if they did not see it regularly twice a day. And evening came, and the lamps were lighted, and Violet did her best to spoil her bright young eyes by reading a 'seaside' novel by the dim light of the high lamp, until Mr. Randolph came—and supper-time.

'Truffled sandwiches, shrimps and tomato
sauce—they sound good,' mused Violet, reading
from the bill of fare. 'I am getting a gour-
mand!' she laughed. 'I do believe that the
dominant thought in my mind for the last hour
has been what I would order for my supper.'

'It's an important question, and there isn't
much else to think of,' said Max Randolph. 'I
recommend pickled oysters.'

His recommendation carried the day against
the rival temptations of the other delicacies on
the *menu*. After supper, when the little portable table had been set and served and cleared,
he took up his seat for the evening in Violet's
section, and the legitimate occupant of that
seat, beholding, discreetly and delicately ab-
sented himself, and made the third in a game
of 'cut-throat euchre' at the other end of the
car, and left the pair of friends to talk the
short evening away in peace and comfort.

Many a time and oft these two had sat
together at dinner, or supper, or luncheon-
party, had ridden, and driven, and danced
together, and perhaps ' sat out ' as many dances
as they had danced; had talked over most
things that are between heaven and earth, nay,
soaring beyond these limits, had discussed
their differing views of heaven itself.

Yet now the sense of being away from
home with Max Randolph, alone with him,
speeding by night and day to a new land, a
new life, under his sole care and escort, seemed
somehow to work a slight but subtle change,
to introduce a new element into their relationship, although this new association was only to
endure for the brief period of the journey South.

Max Randolph was always very attentive
to Violet Preston, yet not at all exclusively so.
He was attentive also to others; perhaps he
flirted more or less with those others; he did

not flirt with Miss Preston; they were simply
good comrades. So frank and fraternal, indeed,
was their friendship that even the curious world
accepted it for just what it was. Few or none
'talked about it,' in the sense of implying that it
was anything more than friendship, nor hinted
at orange-blossoms and bridal bells as a probable
crisis. One hopeless admirer of Miss Preston's,
indeed, naturally suspected that Randolph must
be a fellow-victim—did not see how it could be
otherwise! and one woman had been known to
hint that Violet cherished a secret *tendresse* for
Max; but the world—their little world—in
general let Mr. Randolph and Miss Preston
alone as frankly and simply good friends.

Friendship between man and woman is not
so uncommon as those who are incapable of it
—and they are many—honestly believe it to
be. To some natures, and those often the
most susceptible to other forms of affection, it

is an impossibility, and these naturally set it down as a delusion or a fraud. Violet Preston was one of the women who prove the possibility of such friendship. She could be, and had been, and more than once, as simply good and true and loyal a friend to a man as to a woman; and *how* good a friend Violet could be was known only to a few. First and foremost amongst the few was Rosemary Heath, and possibly amongst them also Max Randolph might be counted; but it was always difficult to find out exactly what Max Randolph knew or thought of anybody, more especially of any woman. It was all but impossible to arrive at the estimate he held in his secret heart of even women in general, still more hopeless to seek to gauge his full and true opinion of any one woman in particular.

Violet Preston knew about as little of Max Randolph as anyone else; she had often wondered whether he was in love with anyone. True, he always declared himself incapable of love, talked of it as of an unknown Debatable Land; but Violet knew him well enough to realise how little he allowed her or anyone else to know of him, and sometimes she marvelled how it was that he managed to be so reserved and yet to seem so frank, that he could talk so much about himself and yet tell so little.

So in the old way the second evening on the cars wore away, and the 'good-night' came, and Violet frankly acknowledged to herself that it had been quite a pleasant day.

The next morning they were still running through flat and monotonous country, having passed through the most picturesque part of the route, the belt of cypress swamps, during the night. Now, however, the red earth of Georgia had given place to the white sand of Florida. White banks and stretches of sand

glared like snow in the morning sun. The
bare skeleton trees of the wintry North, which
had been growing gradually fewer and further
between, now were seen no more ; they had
given place to the evergreen ' yellow pines ' of
the South, unlike their northern brethren, tall
and slim and straight, with their graceful
feathery crowns, so fragile, so erect, it
seems a wonder how those slender stems can
support even that light and airy leafy plume.
Here and there were tropical touches in the
landscape now ; here the grey ' Spanish moss '
of the South hung in long trails from the
branches, and there a palmetto tree stood tall
in its stately grace above the autumn-coloured
brushwood. There seemed something odd and
incongruous in the meeting and mingling of the
palms and the tropical moss and the fresh green
of the young pines with those gold and brown
and russet hues that flecked the underwood.

They passed occasional groups of little wooden cottages, each of which stood up on four or more legs, and the inmates, who all turned out to see the train pass, grew blacker and blacker as they sped further and further south. Little black Topsies, all teeth and eyes, and pigs, all long legs and immense snouts, with very little bacon on their gaunt ribs, tumbled in the mud together.

Presently there was a sudden stoppage, when no station, no settlement, not so much as a shed was in sight to account for it. Incident was scarce on this journey, and two or three gentlemen left the car and went forward along the train to see if peradventure there might be some tiny scrap of excitement to break the monotony, and to give themselves a little prestige by bringing back the news to the select and aristocratic retreat of the 'Pullman Sleeper' which occupied the rear of the train.

It next occurred to two or three of the ladies that there was no particular reason why they too should not go forward and investigate for themselves. Violet was one of these daughters of Eve. They passed forward through a parlour-car, then through an ordinary car, and on, forward still, through a smoking-car—the floor of which was uncarpeted, but its occupants had done their modest best towards carpeting it with orange-peel and banana-skins.

The occupants at present were only a coloured family—a good-humoured father, an ebony mother in a huge bandanna turban, and three or four elfish-looking children—the white passengers having presumably gone with the crowd in search of a sensation, however slight.

Violet followed the other ladies, forward still, and eventually arrived in a baggage car. There was not much baggage in it; but here were some of the passengers of inquiring mind, amongst them Max Randolph; and, looking out of the great open door in the side of the car, Violet saw half-a-dozen or so of the train officials, distinguishable by their uniform, standing round the object of interest—neither more nor less than an unlucky cow, which had been caught up on the cow-catcher, and been carried a mile or so before it had struggled or fallen off.

The poor beast was injured; and there was a discussion going on as to whether it ought or ought not to be killed, and whether the railway company was liable for damages—a discussion far less loud and lively than it would have been in almost any country of Europe. As Violet surveyed the group standing round and debating the matter with characteristic American composure and coolness, she could not help thinking, and remarking to Max Randolph, ' How Frenchmen and Italians would have gesticulated and uplifted their voices and talked all at once !'

The unhappy cow was lying on the bank with its meek head upraised, and looking round with large, wistful, pathetic eyes as if wondering what had happened to it.   Violet Preston, sorry for the poor animal, albeit not emotional nor exclamatory, stepped forward to lean and look closer.   While she stood in the doorway, the train gave a slight preparatory jolt—a very slight one, but as she was standing leaning forward on the extreme edge of the platform, Max Randolph flung his arm lightly round her and drew her back, to save her from the chance of a fall—the floor of the car being of a sufficient height above the ground to make such a fall unpleasant, even if not dangerous.

'Take care, Miss Violet ; it's never safe to stand so near the edge,' he said, drawing her back into the car.

His arm had not been round her for three seconds; it was the merest triviality of a passing incident; yet somehow it did not pass out of Violet's mind so quickly as such a trifle should have done. It left a vague and misty kind of impression—the sum of which was that it was very nice to be taken care of by—somebody—anybody! perhaps especially pleasant when the somebody was a trusted friend and comrade like Max Randolph.

A couple of hours later they arrived in Jacksonville—which may be called the metropolis of Florida, its centre of traffic and commerce, although Tallahassee is its political capital.

With swinging engine-bell clanging out a noisy proclamation of their approach, they dashed through the outskirts of the town, and the great train slackened along the platform of the Jacksonville ' dépôt.' Mr. Randolph loaded himself with Miss Preston's small packages, and they descended from the car into the hubbub of yelling 'touters' for the different hotels. Violet, paying no attention to the babel of 'Everett House!' 'Carlton Hotel!' 'This way for the St. James!' 'Here you are for the boat!' &c., looked out eagerly among the crowd; yet Max Randolph was the first to catch sight of the face she sought.

'There's Miss Rosemary,' he said, as a charming figure slipped quickly through the crowd towards them—followed by many appreciative glances as she passed, the men looking at her face, the women at her dress.

Violet Preston was not a girl of the 'gushing' sort, and Rosemary Heath was still less that way inclined; but their two fair faces flushed and lit up with pure delight as they met, and they kissed each other with hearty whole-souled welcome and affection, while Max Randolph looked on somewhat enviously, and presently observed—

'Really, this sort of thing makes one wish to be a woman!'

# CHAPTER III.

## ON THE ST. JOHN'S RIVER.

' Friendship is constant in all other things
Save in the office and affairs of Love ! '

VIOLET PRESTON and Rosemary Heath, fast
friends since their earliest schooldays, had
always made up their minds that *they* at least
would be constant in those affairs as in all others.
They had been mere children when they made
their pact of friendship, an alliance never yet
broken by even a passing ruffle of disagreement ;
now they were mature young women who had
well attained to years of discretion, and had
both left their first love-stories some years behind ; and no man had ever come between
them ! as they often fondly and proudly said.

Possibly one reason for this satisfactory state of things was that few men who admired the one found much to admire in the other, so opposite were their styles of beauty.

Violet, fair as a lily, with a delicate bloom like the heart of a blush-rose on her cheeks, with deep blue eyes and silky smooth dark hair, was in features, as well as in colouring, a striking contrast to Rosemary, of whom a rival had given the brief but unflattering *signalement*, ' Red hair, black eyes, and tallow cheeks ! ' Certainly her eyes were of a brown so dark it was pardonable for a casual observer to call them black ; her hair, tawny in the shadow, shone red-gold in the light ; and her complexion was of that pure creamy white, without a tinge of pink, which some people call 'waxen,' thereby giving a chance to the hearer to pass the epithet on as ' tallowy ' without too great a strain on conscience.

But there was likeness as well as contrast between the two girls. They were about the same height, and although Violet was a little the slighter and thinner of the two, yet their figures were on the whole sufficiently similar for them to wear each other's jackets and mantles. From long association and affection they had caught one or two tricks of manner and expression alike. They had some similar tastes; they went out sketching together; they sang duets, and played each other's accompaniments; and both had in their schooldays written what it pleased them to call poems. They were fond, though in differing ways and degrees, of romance and novelty, of dress, dancing, and society. And there all likeness ended. Beyond this border-land of sympathetic tastes, their characters, utterly different, were as completely in opposition as the colouring of their hair and eyes.

They had plenty to say to each other now, as they had been separated for some months. Rosemary's parents—that is, her father and stepmother, ' her people,' as she habitually called them—belonged to the large and ever-increasing colony of resident English in Florida; they had, unluckily for her, being tempted by a bargain in the shape of a fine young grove, elected to settle in one of the more sparsely populated parts of the State, where they led a very quiet and lonely life, to Rosemary's exceeding discontent. Fortunately for her, the locality, which certainly lay low and had more swamp around it than is desirable for health, appeared not to agree with her; she had ailed and drooped, and it was arranged that she should spend the winter with her uncle and aunt, Mr. and Mrs. Whitworth, also transplanted Britons, who resided in a healthier part of Florida, and led what seemed by all report to be a much pleasanter life, and with them she was to have the added comfort of her friend Violet's companionship. It was in order to meet Violet on her arrival from the North that Rosemary had joined a party of friends on a trip to Jacksonville.

'I would have come to you at Pine Ridge,' Violet said affectionately.

'Well, I believe you actually would have made even that sacrifice to friendship for me, Vi. But I wouldn't have had you there. Pine *Ridge?* ugh! There isn't a ridge in sight! It's as flat as a tea-tray. I was so miserable there that nothing could have made it much better for *me*, and it would have been all the worse for *you*; there would have been two victims instead of one! What's Max Randolph doing down here?' she added more cheerfully.

'Going to look after orange groves, I believe.'

'Like everyone else here. I wonder how

soon you'll hate the very name of oranges as much as I do?'

'I am very fond of oranges. I don't think I shall hate them very soon.'

'Well, you *are* a more contented disposition—more resigned to life—than I am,' said Rosemary, 'so let us hope you won't get sick of this Sunny South so soon as I did! By the way, how is your little Southern friend, Mamie Otis?'

'Much as usual; and I was just going to tell you she promised to write to greet me here —I told her to address " P.O., Jacksonville." I wonder, have we time to go to the post-office before dinner?'

'Lots of time,' replied Rosemary leisurely. 'Where's Mr. Max? He might go with us, or instead of us. Of course he's off somewhere out of reach—just like a man! Never in the way when he's wanted.'

So without escort, which, however, was not at all needed under the circumstances, the two girls set off to walk to the post-office. Jacksonville is a Southern, but not a very tropical-looking, city; its orange-trees are mostly somewhat stumpy, and its bananas weedy; it is building up fast—so fast that there is an air of sawdust and shavings about it; the loose, deep, heavy sand of which its roads are composed prevents walking from being a pleasure, and makes driving a penalty; but it can boast of beautiful avenues, overarched by splendid evergreen oaks, of pretty and picturesque houses, of hotels and boarding-houses without number, convenient street-cars, and good shops, into the windows of which Rosemary cast interested glances as they passed, though Violet, fresh from New York, was indifferent to their allurements.

Arrived at the post-office, they found, extending from the window whence letters were delivered, half way up the street, a solid *queue* of men, closely packed one behind the other in Indian file, waiting, with the stoical patience of the American, for their letters, and pressing forward slowly, inch by inch, as one after another the foremost of the file obtained their budgets and moved on.

'Oh, Rose!' said Violet with mild dismay, 'it will take us an hour to get up to the window!'

'My dear Vi, it will take us exactly half a minute. Do you forget that we are in the South? Come along!'

And Rosemary coolly took the file in flank, and calmly cut across them to the window, every man making way with respect for the ladies. The foremost man of the procession, who was about to present his card at the window, bowed and drew back, giving place to Violet, so that she got her letter immediately.

'I think,' she observed with a contented smile, as the two girls walked away homewards, 'that I shall enjoy Florida life! I like the Southern ways so much.'

'A little cheap chivalry is all very well,' replied Rosemary, ' but give *me* theatres, shops, good solid bricks and mortar !'

.    .    .    .    .    .    .    .

The great river steamer was holding its steady and stately way southwards, up the St. John's River (which flows north, so that ' down South ' is ' up the river,' which seems unnatural at first to the tourist new to these regions).

It was evening ; the saloon supper was over, and on the deck, amongst many other passengers, sat a well-contented trio, Rosemary, Violet, and Max Randolph. Their ways lay southward still, and still in the same direction, the goal for which he was bound being only a few miles distant from West Grove

House, the residence of Rosemary's relatives.
So here was Mr. Randolph still in attendance.

Miss Heath's friends in Jacksonville had
expressed their satisfaction that the young
ladies should have an old friend of Miss Preston's as escort on their voyage. Violet was
glad; Rosemary, who only found life endurable
with a man or men at hand to offer *petits soins*,
was glad. Max Randolph would have been
less than man if he were not glad to take two
such fair charges under his care; so everybody
was pleased, and a happy trio sat on the deck
in the dusk, Max dividing his devotion pretty
equally between the two girls, as he usually
did—although if the attention he paid to them
were equal in degree, it was different in kind.
There was a flavour of flirtation in his manner
to Rosemary, while to Violet he talked more as
a friend and comrade.

It was a beautiful, balmy Southern night;

they had left the North and the winter far
behind. Great bright 'stars as large as lilies'
were entangled in thin vaporous veils of cloud,
that floated like filmy wreaths in the purple
depths of the sky; like fellow-stars fallen on
the land, the yellow lamps shone out here and
there on the distant shores, as the boat held its
way along the broad majestic river; and from
the tall black funnel showers of red flaming
sparks flashed and flew backwards through the
darkness.

Rosemary and Violet sat leaning against the
bulwarks, looking out across the water at the
far-off lamps and dusky shores. Their escort
had drawn his campstool near to them, so
that he had a good view of the two pale profiles
dimly fair against the sky.

'I don't think anything could be much
better than this,' he observed in a kind of
musing content.

'There are some good hours in life,' said Violet with a little dreamy happy sigh.

'A few!' said Rosemary demurringly.

'A few?' Max Randolph echoed. 'I should have thought *you* found a good many,. Miss Rosemary. It always seems to me that life's a sort of triumphal progress to *you*. Have you been on the war-path lately? How many scalps of the aborigines hang at your girdle?'

'None—for a good reason.'

'Why so?'

'Because the aborigines are bald!' she replied gravely.

'Can't take them by the forelock, eh?' he said.

'You must be getting hungry for a scalp, Rosie,' laughed Violet.

'I am,' she admitted freely; and then suddenly turning to Max, she added—

'Take off your hat!'

Max obeyed, disclosing a sleek dark brown head of hair, not so closely cropped as it might have been.

'I see it's there,' Rosemary observed lightly.

'What's there?'

'Your scalp; it's to be had!'

'For the taking?' suggested Violet.

'No, it isn't,' he replied decidedly. 'It sounds rude to contradict a lady; but how can my scalp be there when you took it long ago, Miss Rosemary? It *seems* to be here; but this is a world where " nothing is, but all things seem." It is only the appearance of a scalp you see!'

'A shadowy triumph,' Violet remarked.

'I'd test its reality if I had a practical tomahawk,' said Rosemary, more briskly than usual.

'Small doubt you would,' he observed drily.

' Hearts are all in your line, Rose,' said her friend, ' but I think you might let *heads* alone ! '

' That's right, Miss Violet ; stand up for me !  Save my head ! ' said Max meekly.

' Nought was never in danger ! ' she laughed ; ' and you said just now that there was no head there ! '

' Have you known me so long, and so well, and not found out that I seldom speak the truth ? '

' I don't know you very well,' demurred Violet.  ' Nobody does, I think.'

' Not Miss Rosemary ? ' he rejoined, with the touch of latent irony in his tone a little more perceptible.

' I never took the trouble to study you,' said Rosemary indolently.  ' I always let sphinxes and riddles alone.'

' I think I'll go overboard and hide my

head!' he observed in mock discomfiture.
'I'm *sure* I would—only I haven't got my life-
preserver on.'

The girls laughed, Rosemary a little scorn-
fully, Violet in the facile rippling mirth of
youth and happiness. Rosemary laughed, as
she spoke, in a rich contralto, unusually deep
for a woman, and sweet as the nightingale's
rich liquid notes. It was a voice not to be
forgotten when once heard, remarkable for its
full *timbre* and its peculiar penetrating sweetness.

The night-breeze was cooling, the evening
wearing on; the deck was being rapidly de-
serted as the passengers retired to their state-
rooms to woo sweet sleep; and Rosemary and
Violet soon followed the example of the majority, leaving Max Randolph almost alone on
the deck.

The girls, of course, had to have their usual

nightly gossip—the ' traditional back-hair chat.'
If they had been talking all day, there would
never fail to be something left over for the last
talk at night. They had to speak low, in order
not to take the occupants of the adjoining
state-rooms into their confidence, and whilst
they simultaneously talked and brushed and
combed their long hair, the limited dimensions
of the apartment which they shared compelled
one to get up and sit on the top berth to keep
out of the other's way.

'Nice having Max with us, isn't it?' said
Violet in her usual frank way. They often
called him 'Max' behind his back, but always
formally 'Mr. Randolph' to his face.

'Yes, it is,' agreed Rosemary as frankly,
adding, in a tone which carried its full weight
of meaning—

'Our Max is *appreciative*!'

'Of *us*?' laughed Violet.

'Yes; it would be no recommendation if he were too appreciative of other people!'

'I think he has a general appreciation of feminine charms in his quiet way,' observed Violet.

'He certainly always seems to find an attraction where *we* are,' said Rosemary.

'He divides his attention pretty fairly, I think,' rejoined Violet, with a little—ever so little—note of interrogation in her tone.

'Yes—it's seldom that a man seems to like us both so equally, so utterly different as we are,' observed Rosemary. 'I sometimes wonder if he admires one of us a little more than the other.'

'Which is it, do you think?' Violet asked, on the impulse of the moment; it was the last thing she had intended to say.

'Didn't you find out on the way down, when you had him all to yourself in the cars?'

'Why, you know Max and I are just good friends, and we only talk like friends,' Violet answered, sincerely enough.

'Shall I find out which he likes best?' Rosemary asked, after a minute's pause.

'If you like,' Violet consented. 'But I don't think Max Randolph's a man to admire anybody over much. He thinks more of himself than of anybody else.'

'No!' exclaimed Rosemary, with sardonic surprise. 'Astonishing man! *rara avis* among his sex! Thinks of himself before anybody else, does he? Why, Vi, he ought to be

> Painted upon a pole, and under-writ,
> Here you may see—a marvel!'

'I don't think as badly of men as you do, Rose,' said Vi.

'All the worse for you, my child,' interposed her friend.

'I have known good men and true,' Violet
continued staunchly.   'I think men are as
faithful and good as women—sometimes!'

'So are swans black and roses blue—sometimes,' retorted Rosemary.

Meanwhile the subject of their conversation
was sitting not far off from them in the saloon,
absorbed in a conversation of his own with a
fellow-passenger, although they did not hear
his voice, for Max Randolph, like many of his
countrymen, habitually spoke in a subdued
tone.   He was 'talking Florida' from a business
point of view, as a field for investment, discuss-
ing the probabilities of profits to be derived
from groves, town-lots, railways, and so forth,
with one of the 'land agents' who are as sands
upon the sea-shore in Florida, who naturally
regard every tourist as a possible investor.
This gentleman had scented almost at once in
Max Randolph one more of that numerous

class of travellers he knew so well, and whose ways and means it was part of his business to study—another of the men who come South to 'look round,' and see if there is anything to be picked up on Tom Tiddler's ground, and generally find that there is nothing whatever to be 'picked up,' but something to be got by dint of hard digging.

Like the majority of men who go to Florida, regarding it with any other eyes than those of the mere pleasure-tourist or health-seeker, Max Randolph had not much money, and he wanted to make some somehow. Another, although secondary, object he had, the pursuance of his art. He intended to make sketches and studies of Florida scenery. Thus much Violet Preston knew, in common with the rest of his friends. Indeed, she knew as much as most of them, no more, and no less. She knew the main facts of his history.

Southern born and bred, with a good share of Southern pride, a passion for art, and an empty purse, he had moved to Boston too late to be entirely convinced of the centrality of 'the hub of the universe'; early enough to pick up some Boston ways of thought, and a fair amount of Boston literary culture, though even in his happiest days there he never failed to feel that 'There is a world elsewhere!' Then he went out West, where he perceived still more clearly the far-sweeping scope of the world outside, and realised more and more fully, as day by day he looked upon the boundless expanse of the rolling prairie and heaven-scaling peaks of the snow-topped mountains, the vast and all but limitless range of Life and Nature; and the civilised 'world' of his youth gradually grew less in his eyes, till it seemed but a little island in the vast sea of life.

There, in the great, wild, free West, he

tried his hand in the mines, and on the ranches, lived among hunters, gold-diggers, cattle-men, roved as they roved, and, like them, carried his life in his hand, his revolver in his pocket, wore his hair long and his boots above his knees.

Although, after a time, he gave up this nomad existence—the mines having yielded *him* no gold—and returned to civilisation, still the memory of that dip into the wild, free life of the frontier abided with him ; its aroma clung round him and took its part in the moulding of his character, and to it he often looked back as not the least agreeable of the mixed experiences of his roving life.

Next he determined to spend a few years in the Old World, studying art. He went to England, where he was well received—nay more, it may fairly be said that he was petted

and made much of, as an American is apt to
be, and where he first met and made friends
with Violet Preston. He had a couple of
pictures hung in the Royal Academy; then,
satisfied with his success, he moved on to Paris
and to Rome, as a good American is bound to
do; and Max Randolph's studio became, for
the season, a place to visit in each city. In
time he paid another passing visit to London,
on his way back to New York, where he and
Miss Preston met again, and where he took up
his quarters for awhile. He had no real home,
but made himself at home everywhere, and
was as settled in New York as he would have
been anywhere else, until the roving fit seized
him again, and took the shape of the Florida
fever; and, viewing the orange groves in the
double light of landscapes and investments, he
packed his portmanteau and started off.

Thus much everybody knew of him; and

it was about all that anybody knew. Everything that concerned his private life, and his loves—if he had any—remained under lock and key; and no one yet had picked the lock nor found the key.

# CHAPTER IV.

## WEST GROVE HOUSE.

WEST GROVE HOUSE was one of the many establishments in Florida, whose advertisements, figuring in our London papers, offer an answer to the vexed question, 'What to do with our Boys?'—one of the places where young Englishmen are taken in and done for—that is, are taught practical orange culture, if they will learn, and put in the way of making good bargains in land, if they will buy. Mr. Whitworth was one of the 'real estate agents' whose name is legion in Florida. He had plenty of land to sell on commission, and was willing to let his young friends have the benefit of his advice in the matter of purchase. Also, as he had a house too large for himself and wife, he furnished them with board and lodging for a reasonable consideration.

West Grove House was a big wooden, barrack-like building, run up in the usual Southern style, with ample open-air accommodation in the shape of broad piazzas running round three sides of it, and balconies above the piazzas, so that no one need ever be driven to sit indoors unless they chose. Its foundations, of course, were above instead of under ground, a platform resting on timber supports three or four feet high, affording room for the playful earthquake to give a roll and heave beneath it with as little damage as possible, and also room for broken bottles, old tin cans, and rubbish of all sorts, to be thrown under the house, besides still leaving room for the suggestion, to nervous temperaments, of a spacious and safe retreat for tramps, lunatics, and mad dogs.

The house stood in the midst of an orange grove, of course, and, equally of course, it was close to a lake. In that land of lakes, the Orange belt of Florida, no one would invest as much capital as was represented by West Grove House and its surrounding grounds, unless the site of the estate was near a lake. Indeed, West Grove House was favoured by the proximity of four lakes ; it lay within easy reach of one of the great lakes of the country; it fronted on a middle-sized lake, and had a back view of two little lakes.

The room allotted to Violet and Rosemary was a large corner room, with two windows at right angles, from one of which they had a view, across the orange grove and a fringe of pine-trees, to the South lake, and from the other, across a wider stretch of grove, to a thicker wood of pine-trees, through which in the distance broke silvery gleams of the largest lake.

There was no garden; the house was simply set down in the middle of the grove. There were no flower-borders, and the scanty grass which qualified the level stretch of sand in front of the house to be raised to the dignity of a 'lawn' looked unhappy, brown and sallow and sickly; any respectable British cow would have disdained its quality; while as for quantity, there was a good deal more sand than grass— the usual white Florida sand. Except on the south side of the house, there was no grass at all. North and east and west the white sand had it all its own way. The white sandy soil of the Florida pine-lands is by no means so poor and barren as it looks. It might be mistaken for mere desert sea-sand by a superficial glimpse; but, scratch that sun-bleached surface, and a layer of richer soil lies underneath, and in this white sand the orange groves flourish.

The trees, scattered at intervals of some thirty or forty feet around West Grove House, were all in splendid condition, their foliage of a deep, rich, glossy green, their branches bowed down beneath the weight of ruddy ripe golden fruit.

'How beautiful they look!' exclaimed Violet admiringly. 'I do think an orange-tree is the loveliest of trees. And what a pretty view altogether!'

'Yes, it's pretty for a day,' said Rosemary. 'It's prettier than *our* place; and then a view always does seem prettier when you and I see it together. But even with you, Vi, I shan't admire this landscape very long. After all, it's only the regular Florida outlook—flat as a tea-tray—oranges, pine-trees, lake; lake, pine-trees, oranges—the sort of thing that always ought to have sunset or moonlight turned on it.'

'Well, we shall have sunsets and moonlight,' Violet replied cheerfully; ' but, " for mine own poor part," I think it looks pretty well in the morning sunshine. I fancy I shall be a long time tiring of it. I like the house, too; everything looks so sweet and clean and comfortable.'

Here Mrs. Whitworth made her appearance —a comely matron, still on the right side of middle-age, with a certain likeness to her lovely niece, Rosemary, in general features, in the shape of her dark eyes, and the growth and wave of her hair. But the hair was nut-brown, without a tinge of the red-gold sheen of Rosemary's; the face it shaded was larger, fuller, squarer, than Rosemary's tapering oval, which 'lessened in perfect cadence' from broad low brow to dainty chin; and the expressions of aunt and niece were entirely different. There was nothing dreamy, nothing unrestful, nothing languid, in Mrs. Whitworth's keen, kindly eyes, firm, good-humoured mouth, and brisk energy of manner.

'Well, girls, are you nearly ready for dinner?' she inquired. The visitors had only that morning reached West Grove House, and had not yet left their room, to which they had been straightway shown on their arrival, and where they had been resting a little, unpacking a little, and, of course, talking all the time. Only that morning, too, their ways and Max Randolph's had parted, but he was not very far off; he had repaired to the home of a lately-settled friend, a few miles the other side of the South Lake, with whom he intended taking up his quarters, at least for a time.

Mrs. Whitworth found the girls quite ready for dinner, and for the introduction to the other members of the household, none of whom, with the exception of Mr. Whitworth, they had yet seen, and concerning whom they cherished some mild curiosity.

A dozen young men were hanging about the large, bare, central hall, which ran from the front door to the back door of West Grove House, various sitting and sleeping, dining and smoking rooms opening off either side of it; and as Mrs. Whitworth, followed by the two new arrivals, descended the stairs, there was a general doffing of hats—hats amongst which, as Violet observed, the 'chimney-pot,' beloved of the British heart, was the only style unrepresented. There were wideawakes, Glengarrys, billycocks, Panamas—anything and everything but the familiar 'chimney-pot' of home.

'Ah, my hungry flock, all ready and waiting?' exclaimed Mrs. Whitworth. Immediately, at the sound of her voice, there was a prodigious trampling and clattering on the bare boards, as in from the south piazza, and in from the east piazza, and in from the back-yard, came trooping more young men, at least a dozen more. The whole company filed in after the ladies, and took their seats at a long table which extended from end to end of the large dining-room. Mrs. Whitworth placed the two girls one on either side of Mr. Whitworth, and took her own seat at the side, about the middle of the table, where she could, as she remarked, 'command the situation.'

Personal and particular introduction of the newcomers to so large a party was of course impossible; but, while the soup was being served, Mrs. Whitworth performed a perfunctory kind of presentation of her guests to their immediate neighbours.

'Mr. Conyers, my niece, Miss Heath; and Miss Preston, Mr. Tregelva.'

Whereon the young men addressed bowed low, and the girls smiled their sweetest.

After the soup, came fish—fried black bass, and an excellent fish too.

'Staples caught this, didn't he?' said Mr. Whitworth.

A voice halfway down the table was heard, in a modest and somewhat melancholy intonation, to disclaim the honour.

'Christie caught it. I was lying in the bottom of the boat.'

There was a laugh at this; evidently lying in the bottom of the boat was considered an eminently characteristic position for the speaker.

Then a large dish, on which reposed a fine roast bird resembling a turkey, was placed upon the table.

'You won't guess what *this* is, Miss Preston?' said the host.

' An ostrich ? ' Violet hazarded a conjecture.

' It's a sand-crane. The butcher didn't come to-day, and Mrs. Whitworth was in despair because there was nothing to eat. Luckily, Tregelva shot this crane. I hope you'll find it good.'

' Sand-crane is very good,' observed Mr. Tregelva. ' White crane isn't; but the grey sand-crane is a good eating bird.'

And indeed the sand-crane was pronounced excellent, having a flavour between a pheasant and a turkey. It was a fine large bird, too, which was lucky, as it was the *pièce de résistance*—the only other viand perceptible to the naked eye being a very scraggy bone of beef —literally a bone—which reposed on a side-table.

For dessert they had oranges, of course.

' I meant to have had some guavas to-day,' Mrs. Whitworth remarked. ' Never mind;

we'll have some after our coffee. It isn't the thing, of course; but I don't see why fruit shouldn't taste as good after coffee as before.'

Dessert over, the party flocked out on to the south piazza, all but a few of them, for whom the smoking-room had greater charms than sunshine and feminine society. The piazza was long and wide, and liberally supplied with armchairs, rocking-chairs, and folding-chairs, besides a hammock and a swing-chair suspended from the roof. In these various seats the regiment of young men promptly disposed themselves, gallantly leaving three of the easiest rocking-chairs in a group for the ladies.

The piazza looked across the lawn, dotted with orange-trees starred with their golden fruit, past a fringe of tall slim pines, oleander and magnolia-trees, to the blue, shining lake; the sun's blaze was tempered by a gentle, balmy breeze, and light gossamer veils of cloud floated in the azure depths of the sky. The chairs were very comfortable; the coffee, which was presently handed round, was very good; the young men were most of them of personable and prepossessing appearance—taking a general view of them, they were a 'well set-up,' manly, and gentlemanly-looking company. Altogether the two girls felt, and had sufficient cause for feeling, content.

'Now for our guavas!' said Mrs. Whitworth. 'Who'll go across to the East Grove and pick them? Don't all speak at once!' she added somewhat drily. The advice was unnecessary, if not ironical; the company manifested not the slightest inclination to 'all speak at once.'

'Staples, you go!' the hostess added after a pause, turning upon a young man who was lying rather than sitting in a limp attitude, with his head sunk forward on his breast, in a reclining chair.

'Hadn't Tregelva better go?' this gentleman demurred. 'Tregelva's fond of guavas.'

'Ye—yes,' assented Mr. Tregelva, who had a soft, slow, drawling intonation, ' but it spoils the flavour unless some other fellow picks them.'

'Quite so,' agreed Mrs. Whitworth. 'Therefore, somebody please go.'

'I'll go,' said a tall young fellow, with dark laughing eyes and a good-humoured mouth, rising with unexpected alacrity.

'That's right, Christie. Staples, you go and help him!' said the lady autocratically. Mr. Staples yielded ; he gathered himself up with a reluctant but resigned air from the luxurious depths of his lounging-chair, and went.

'You haven't got your flock in very good training, Aunt Emma,' observed Rosemary *sotto voce* ; ' there is not what I should call a *stampede* to execute your bidding.'

' Rather cruel, Miss Heath,' languidly interposed Mr. Tregelva, whose ears apparently were long; 'it doesn't take *three* to pick guavas.'

' They do what they're told,' Mrs. Whitworth replied with brisk decisiveness to Rosemary's remark. ' They *have to.* Some of them require a good deal of telling.'

' Mrs. Whitworth,' said a handsome young man, looking up leisurely and speaking without a smile, ' when have you told me to do anything that I haven't done it ? '

' Don't be argumentative, Conyers ! ' she replied ; ' that's your great fault.'

A general laugh attested that this had hit a blot.

Presently Messrs. Christie and Staples returned with a basket of guavas, both looking very warm, Christie smiling, Staples depressed. Mr. Tregelva was dispatched to fetch plates and fruit-knives, and, probably anxious to redeem the general character of the company, hastened cheerfully on the errand.

The guavas were excellent, fresh and ripe, looking like peachy-cheeked apples, but with a delicious flavour all their own, when the ruddy-golden rind was cut through into the luscious, pink and creamy pulp within, which seemed still warm from the sun's kiss. They were the first fresh guavas gathered from the tree which Violet had ever tasted, and even this trifling detail added a pleasing touch to a situation which, she and Rosemary had already made up their minds, was an agreeable one. To Violet there was additional satisfaction in the reflection that her friend, Max Randolph, was not far off—only on the other side of that lake—and that he would probably call to pay his respects that evening. Nor was this reflection altogether indifferent to Rosemary. Max would be one man the more, and one who already appreciated her charms.

In the evening—that is to say, soon after the six o'clock tea, which, with one o'clock dinner, was the order of the day at West Grove House—Mr. Randolph duly put in an appearance, and was introduced to Mrs. Whitworth, and made himself agreeable to her according to his lights—not that general agreeability was by any means Max Randolph's *forte* ; but though he seldom said pretty things or civil things, or put himself at all out of his way to please, there were very few women who did not like Max Randolph, and Mrs. Whitworth was evidently going to be no exception to the rule.

The ladies were in the parlour, as a light shower and rising breeze made the piazza somewhat cool and damp for a lounging-place. The parlour was large, white-walled, white-ceiled, simply furnished, and scantily ornamented, but comfortable and home-like. All the chairs were easy ; books and papers lay about temptingly on the tables, and there was a piano, and a goodly pile of music.

The girls had unpacked their trunks and changed their travelling-dresses. They generally chose their toilettes so as to harmonise, and never ' killed ' each other's colours. This evening Violet was what Rosemary affectionately called ' a little pigeon '—that is to say, she had on a soft dove-coloured dress, simply and gracefully made, with knots of blue ribbon nestling here and there ; while Rosemary wore a robe of some clinging cream-coloured material, relieved with touches of a warm red-brown, not unlike the darker shades in her own rich hair—this harmony of tints was a little daring, but very effective and becoming, as Rosemary's toilettes always were.

Mrs. Whitworth, surveying the two girls approvingly, reflected that they were an exceedingly attractive addition to her establishment.

'And how did you get here ?' Violet inquired conversationally of Max Randolph.

'Martin drove me round the lake in his buggy ; he's gone on to some place near here —said he'd call for me on his way home, if you will let me inflict myself on you for an hour or so ?' turning to Mrs. Whitworth.

'We shall be only too glad of your company, Mr. Randolph,' that lady protested cordially.

'Although we have already a score of your noble sex on the premises, there's always room and a welcome for one more,' observed Rosemary.

'Even when the one is you,' said Violet, who often had her saucy fling at Max Randolph ; and their light and laughing glances met with the usual familiar freedom—more freely now than during the days they had been virtually alone on the journey South.

' " Will you walk into my parlour ? said the spider to the fly," ' Rosemary sang softly and smilingly. ' But *your* flies don't seem inclined to walk into the parlour, Aunt Em. Are they afraid of being eaten up ? '

' Where *are* all your friends and countrymen ? ' Mr. Randolph inquired, having not as yet seen so much as the whisk of a coat-tail of the ' Household Brigade.'

' Countrymen they are, and friends they shall be ; but we have not made much progress towards friendship yet,' replied Rosemary.

' As for me, I haven't yet got any one of

them labelled with his proper name,' said Violet.

'Haven't made much impression, eh?' remarked Max.

'Not *yet*,' Violet smiled.

'Oh, I do remember,' she added, 'the one with the long nose, who always pokes his chin on his breast and dives his hands deep in his pockets, is Mr. Staples.'

'Fascinating description!' commented Max. 'I don't think I'll mind *him*!'

'Which is the good-looking fair one who never speaks?' inquired Rosemary.

'Conyers? Why, my dear child, he opened his mouth three times this afternoon, and made three distinct and articulate remarks. That's a great deal for him!'

'And the tall slight one, with the little dark moustache, who fetched the plates for the fruit?'

'Oh, Christie! Christie is a sweet boy, we're very fond of him,' replied Mrs. Whitworth, who called all her flock by their surnames as freely as a schoolmaster addresses his class.

Here Mr. Whitworth came in; and, immediately scenting in Max Randolph a possible purchaser of a grove, within ten minutes had invited him to drive out the next day and inspect some highly desirable land which he, Mr. Whitworth, held for disposal at a rate which made it 'A bargain, I do assure you, my dear sir, a rare bargain; and when you see it you will say so.'

Then Mrs. Whitworth opened the piano, and asked the girls to sing. Violet pleaded a slight cold in her throat; and Rosemary, who liked an audience, the while

> Her fingers wandered idly
> Over the ivory keys,

inquired :—

'Aunt Emma, don't your little flock ever come in of an evening?'

'I'll call them,' said Mrs. Whitworth; and going out into the hall and across to the smoking-room she gave a general invitation, in a tone that suggested a royal command. 'Come in, all of you, or some of you; we're going to have a little music. Come and be audience.'

At this summons Mr. Christie and Mr. Staples came promptly, and after them a half-dozen others strayed in one by one, and lined the walls and hung around the door. None, except Mr. Tregelva and young Christie, penetrated as far into the room as the centre table, nor ventured upon the occupation of any chairs save those which were in safe retirement, backed against the wall. Apparently, the lack of feminine society at West Grove House had rendered them a little shy of it. Thus Rose-

mary and her friend had not much opportunity
of progress in the matter of identification,
although, before the end of the evening, they
had succeeded in 'placing' Mr. Tregelva, with
his fair, close-cropped head, long tawny moustache, and sleepy-looking pale-blue eyes, who
distinguished himself by volunteering to fetch
in another lamp, and who acted as the mouth-
piece of the general desire when any especial
song was requested, and who also led the
chorus of the murmured applause, which never
rose above a murmur.

Rosemary was in splendid voice, and she
sang her songs of sweetest sentiment, of most
sparkling gaiety, of most tragic pathos; but
she was compelled to admit in confidence to
Violet that 'she had sung to more enthusiastic
audiences.'

'They will warm up,' Violet said con-
solingly; 'the fact is, Rosie, you and I have

become so used to American expansion and demonstrativeness, we really don't know what to make of British reserve.'

'I think they are shy,' observed Rosemary demurely, 'and probably require a little gentle encouragement.'

'And there's small fear that they will not have it,' said Violet laughing, as the two friends, with affectionately linked arms—a prettier picture than West Grove House had seen for many a day—went their way to their room.

'I never come down to breakfast, my dears,' Mrs. Whitworth said as she bade them good-night. 'I have a cup of tea in bed. You two can do just what you like; the breakfast bell will ring at seven—but have your breakfast in bed if you like.'

Neither Rosemary nor Violet did like, however. They preferred a good sociable breakfast at table to cups of tea in bed, and at the

summons of the seven o'clock bell they were
as nearly ready to go down as could reason-
ably be expected. The bell not only rang
punctually, but continued ringing at intervals
of three or four minutes. Violet hurried the
finishing touches to her toilette, but in vain, as
Rosemary declined to hasten, and Violet waited
for her. When they went down to the dining-
room, they found the long table full, and the
whole regiment at breakfast; it looked like a
barrack mess; and all the troop rose up in
respectful greeting, with a mighty pushing and
scraping of chairs on the bare floor.

'Are we late?' Violet asked apologetically,
as she slipped into the chair which Mr. Tregelva
placed for her.

'How many bells do they ring?' inquired
Rosemary; 'I counted seven.'

'Oh, they go on ringing till everybody's
down,' Mr. Staples replied.

Meanwhile, Mr. Christie had hastened to the side-table to pour out some coffee for the ladies. Mr. Tregelva followed him to cut some ham for them, and Mr. Conyers very leisurely brought up the rear with bread and butter. Mr. Whitworth had already finished his breakfast and left the table; the smart young mulatto who officiated as indoor 'factotum' did not 'wait' at breakfast, but Violet and Rosemary had never found themselves so well waited upon before. The young men were one and all ready to jump up and hasten to the side-table in their behalf. Even Mr. Staples, looking, as usual, limp and loose-jointed, with his large, mild, melancholy eyes, and his habitual depression of aspect, got up to fetch them a piled-up platter, with the tempting invitation, 'Won't you have some hot cakes? they're quite cold.'

The day began well; but, as it went on, the girls did not find it blest with so much of social

and congenial communion as might have been
hopefully anticipated from so fair a beginning,
and a fear began to dawn on them that possibly,
amongst this gallant band, there might prove to
be no congenial souls to commune with. Almost
immediately after breakfast the party scattered.
Messrs. Conyers and Tregelva, with fishing-rods
over their shoulders and tin bait-cans in their
hands, bent their steps in the direction of the
big lake. Young Christie and the two Fraser
brothers set off on a shooting expedition. Mr.
Staples went to fetch the mail from the nearest
post-town; the rest of the brigade dispersed themselves in various directions—none of them were
to be seen about parlour or piazza or grounds.
After the midday dinner, Mr. Whitworth took a
couple of them off to inspect some neighbour-
ing orange groves; he picked up Max Randolph on the round, and having shown him—
in vain—some tempting bargains in the way

of 'wild pine-land,' brought him home to supper.

Conversation as a fine art did not flourish much at West Grove House. It ran entirely on 'oranges and lemons,' groves, 'lots,' and land, 'lake fronts,' wild land, pine-land, bay-land, hammock-land. Violet, who always liked to enter into and take a part in the life of those amongst whom she found herself, took some interest in inquiring which of these various lands were the best, the cheapest, the dearest; why 'lake-fronts' were deemed so desirable, and so on. Rosemary felt no interest at all in the 'land question,' indeed, frankly averred herself to be 'dead tired' of it, and very little in her aunt's gossip—running chiefly on which of the young men had already bought land, which of them were in process of negotiation, and which had not as yet seen anything to suit them—this latter class being by far the largest.

Mrs. Whitworth spoke in kindly terms of her 'little flock.' 'They're a fine set of young fellows,' she observed, 'nearly all of them of the best families. There's Tregelva, an eldest son—Tregelva Hall is a perfectly splendid place, but heavily encumbered—Tregelva's heir to the estate, but he'll have very little means to keep it up. There's Chadwick, Sir Gervase Chadwick's youngest son; and Christie, Lord Court-Royal's nephew; and Staples, he was always looked upon as the Earl of Kilvastone's heir—the old earl was Staples's uncle, a widower, with only two daughters— when what did the old uncle do but go and marry again, and didn't die till he had two sons! Consequently, here is poor Staples. Oh, there's plenty of *sang azur* among them, but very little money—else they wouldn't be here.'

# CHAPTER V.

## THE HOUSEHOLD BRIGADE.

'Mr. Conyers, do you sleep very soundly, or are you the most popular member of this brotherhood?' inquired Rosemary, as she and Violet sat at their social breakfast with the 'Household Brigade'—Messrs. Tregelva, Christie, and Staples vying with each other in ministering to the needs of the fair guests in the direction of ham, fish, toast, and coffee.

'Why do you ask that, Miss Heath?' rejoined Conyers, who liked to know the why and the wherefore of everything. He did not talk much, but the little he did say was generally in a note of interrogation.

'Because you always seem to be in demand at an unearthly hour in the morning,' she replied. 'Every morning we hear your name called upon——'

'We might say *shouted*, in stentorian tones,' Violet observed.

'And we hear a sound,' continued Rosemary, 'suggestive of boots or a broomstick aimed at your door.'

An explosion of mirth from the side-table, where Christie was endeavouring to scrape some meat off a huge ham-bone, testified to his exceeding enjoyment of Miss Heath's observation.

'We call Conyers to come and bathe with us,' said Tregelva.

'He requires a good deal of calling,' Violet remarked.

'I always answer at the first call. It's very seldom indeed they have to call me twice,' replied Conyers, handsome, stolid, and literal.

'We bathe every morning in the lake,' observed Staples.

'Without fear of alligators?' she asked.

'Conyers shot a 'gator there week before last—a fellow five feet long,' said young Chadwick, putting in his word.

'I don't count that shooting him. I didn't get him ; he sank.'

'You hit him though. I believe he went down as dead as mutton,' said Tregelva.

'Some of his avenging kindred will have you one day,' remarked Rosemary.

'Grab you by the leg, Conyers !' prophesied Staples, apparently enjoying the idea.

'And down you'll go !' added Tregelva.

'I'm not afraid of 'gators,' rejoined Conyers, who seemed to be paying less attention to the conversation than to a tough piece of ham, at which he was sawing away with a very blunt knife. 'Nobody thinks anything of a 'gator here.'

'*I* thought a good deal of them when I took Mrs. Johnson's girls out on Lake Rosalie in a boat that turned out to leak like a sieve. I thought those alligators were going to have a feast,' said Tregelva.

'An alligator five feet long could pull you under, couldn't he?' asked Violet.

'I suppose he could, if he got hold of you by the leg,' was the reply. 'But one never hears of any accidents. They're not like the Nile crocodiles.'

The subject of alligators being presently exhausted, the two girls, having finished their breakfast, rose up, the regiment all rising with them as one man; and Christie and Staples making a simultaneous move forward to open the door, Christie, of course, attaining the goal first.

'Doesn't it make you feel rather like royalty?' said Violet, in a laughing *aside* to

Rosemary as they crossed the hall towards the piazza, a great trampling and scuffling of feet attesting that the whole of the brigade were swarming in their wake.

'I doubt if royalty appreciates the pleasures of the position half as much,' remarked Rosemary. 'How the sun glares! Let us go up and fetch our crowns, else we shall get our noses burnt brown.'

'And have to drop our sceptres,' added Violet.

They ran upstairs laughing, and got out their broad-brimmed sun-hats; Rosemary tried hers on, and, not being entirely satisfied that it was becoming, refused to go out until she had altered the arrangement of the ribbon and flower.

Hats or parasols, or both, were indeed necessary to all who were mindful of their complexions, for, although it was but little past nine o'clock when the girls returned downstairs, the sun already poured a level blaze straight on to the broad, high, open south piazza, which was the most popular resort.

Not a breath of air stirred the foliage of the tall, slim 'yellow pines,' whose graceful feathery plumes were traced in delicate pencilling against the burning azure of a sky almost too dazzling in its light and colour. The lake, seen in glimpses between and beyond the pine-trees, was as intense and pure a blue as the shining sky above. The shadows of the orange-trees reached long dark fingers across the brownish lawn towards the house. The fruit hung ripe and ruddily golden in the sunshine amongst the deep green glossy leafage. Here and there were lemon-trees starred with their paler fruit; here a mass of branches bent low beneath the weight of enormous citrons; and here a stately tree stood laden with the huge pale golden clusters of the 'grape-fruit,' which looks like an immense lemon-coloured orange or orange-shaped lemon, and has a delicious tart flavour, between the two. The dogs lay like dead dogs, with flaccid ears and inert tails, their passive sides turned up to bask in the sun.

On the edge of the piazza Messrs. Christie and Tregelva were seated, very busy cleaning their guns. Along the broad shallow steps that led down to the lawn Mr. Staples stretched his length, his hat pulled well over his eyes, the tip of his nose recklessly exposed to sunburn. Mr. Conyers was reposing in a rocking-chair; a second. chair was arranged so as to afford a comfortable resting-place for his manly limbs; a third chair, drawn conveniently up to his right hand, supported his tobacco-pouch, matches, and a yellow paper-covered French novel. He looked as if, save for the trouble of pulling at his meerschaum, he would have been asleep;

Staples, to all appearance, *was* asleep, Tregelva and Christie absorbed in their arsenal
work, when with a soft *frou-frou* of their summer dresses, Violet and Rosemary stepped out
on the piazza.

Conyers lifted his handsome blue eyes heavily, as if the raising of their long lashes were
an effort. Staples's eyes were buried in his hat,
Christie's and Tregelva's fixed on their guns,
until Rosemary made a remark, with a sweet
and genial smile, on the beauty of the morning,
at which the four looked up.

Staples lazily tilted his hat up from his nose,
and then as lazily gathered himself up from his
step and leant against a column, with his head
sunk forward on his breast, and his hands
buried as deep as they would go in his pockets.
Conyers, knocking the ashes leisurely from his
pipe, bethought himself of observing, in an only
slightly interrogative accent, ' You don't mind

smoke?' He evidently would have been very
much taken aback had he received anything
but the cordial assurance that they did *not*,
which Violet promptly gave him.

Seeing Violet about to move her chair back
out of the sun-glare, Staples took his hands out
of his pockets to assist her; and then it occurred
to Conyers to remove his feet from the chair
whereon they were so luxuriously reposing.
Christie and Tregelva put up their guns and
drew near and joined the group, disposing
themselves comfortably in lounging-chairs,
while Staples, having done his duty, got into
the hammock and lay down.

Presently the two Fraser brothers and
young Chadwick came out of the house in an
eminently sportsmanlike 'get-up,' with their
guns over their shoulders and cartridge-belts
round their waists; and with a brisk business
air, which contrasted with the supine attitude

of utter *dolce far niente* of the group on the piazza, they crossed the lawn and turned off down the road. Harrington—a smooth-cheeked stripling, in a suit that looked as if it were made out of a blue and white check duster—lounged out behind them, and stood about aimlessly on the steps. None of the party seemed at all able to make up their minds what to do, or whether to do anything. Tregelva intimated that he regarded 'loafing' as on the whole a more satisfactory occupation than any other.

'Who's going to fetch the mail?' inquired Conyers.

'Spencer's going.'

'Are you going shooting?' asked Harrington.

'N—no, I think not,' Tregelva replied slowly. 'Conyers and I went shooting the other day—were out nearly all day, and we got one miserable quail and a rabbit. They *talk* of sport here. I've more sport out of my own window at home!'

'You can pot an alligator or bag a sand crane—for our dinners!' said Christie.

'And very good the crane was,' observed Violet.

'I'm glad you liked the crane, Miss Preston. Pinkie roasted it very well.'

'Why don't they have dogs?' demanded Staples languidly from his hammock. 'Could get some sport if we had dogs.'

'They haven't got such a thing out here, my dear fellow.'

Here Christie rose up, stretched himself, and announced that he was going to drive to Johnson's Grove in his wagon, and inquired if 'any of you fellows' had a mind to go with him?

Apparently nobody cared to drive to Johnson's Grove, for nobody offered to move.

'There doesn't seem to be anything to do here, nor anywhere to go,' observed Rosemary.

'No, there isn't anywhere—much,' replied Tregelva. 'There's a—a shop—they call it a " dry-goods store " here—about seven miles off, where you can get things——'

'Ladies' things,' added Staples explanatorily, as Tregelva appeared too somnolent to continue.

'What *are* ladies' things?' asked Rosemary gravely.

Staples was for a moment posed by this question; then a brilliant idea flashed upon him, and he replied:

'Well, gloves.'

'Yes, I see you don't wear any,' remarked Rosemary, glancing at the sun-browned hand that hung listlessly over the edge of the hammock.

'And—a—dresses—and bonnets,' continued

Staples, brightening. 'Mrs. Whitworth bought a hat there for fifty cents—that straw thing she wears.'

'It's not polite to call a lady's hat a " thing," drawled Tregelva.

'No, it's a " creation!" ' suggested Harrington.

'You can sell as well as buy in these happy latitudes,' Tregelva continued conversationally, waking up a little. 'Staples has got a coat he's trading with a nigger.'

'We're good traders, both of us,' Staples observed meditatively; 'the nigger pretends he doesn't want to buy, and I make out I don't particularly care to sell.'

'Why don't you throw in those boots of yours?' suggested Conyers.

'Mr. Staples seems to have a great many superfluous articles in his wardrobe,' remarked Violet.

'The boots *are* superfluous,' Staples admitted dejectedly. 'I gave four guineas for them.'

'And I'd let the darkey have them for two dollars if I were you,' said Conyers.

'You should get him to show them to you, Miss Preston,' said Tregelva.

As this manner of mild chaff at each other's expense involved no strain upon the intellect, and thus was eminently qualified to suit the speakers—especially on a tropical morning like this—it ran round the circle, and found fresh targets in Harrington's hat—which may have had a shape originally, but, through long compression in his pocket and flattening in his portmanteau, had lost such form as it had ever possessed—and Tregelva's dust-coloured alpaca suit, against which there was launched the terrible accusation that he had bought it ready-made.

' I wish my tailor could see it!' he observed, casting down his eyes in impartial criticism on his own garments. 'He'd never make me a coat again!'

'He'll never have the chance, if you buy that grove in Tohopekaliga,' said Staples.

'Are you all going to buy groves?' asked Violet.

'That's what we've all come out here for,' Tregelva replied.

'*I* shan't buy unless I see a better grove at a lower price than has been offered me yet,' came a growl from the hammock.

'Have you chosen your grove?' asked Rosemary, lifting her lovely indolent dark eyes to Mr. Tregelva.

'N—no—I've looked at some,' he replied languidly.

'And you, Mr. Conyers?' and the dark eyes turned their beauty on him.

'I don't know. There's no hurry,' said Conyers, whose classically handsome features were hard to stir from their sleepy and bovine sort of calm.

'Oh, Harrington!' shouted Mr. Whitworth from the distance. Nobody lives long in the South without contracting the habit of prefixing an emphatic '*Oh!*' to the name of anyone. '*Oh*, Tregelva! Harrington! Don't you want to come and see John Ross? He's just brought in a cartful of deer.'

The whole company rose up *en masse*, even Staples slowly preparing to tumble out of his hammock.

'Anything to *see?*' exclaimed Rosemary, rising with some alacrity. 'Come along, Vi!'

'Stampede in search of the smallest excitement,' remarked Violet, as the whole party hastened helter-skelter into the house and through the hall, that being the shortest cut to the back-yard, where they found indeed a cart, laden—alas! not with the picturesque remains of the antlered monarchs of the forest, but with the same cut up into saddles and haunches, looking very much like an ordinary butcher's cart. The driver, the mighty hunter who had brought in his spoils from the chase, a mahogany-faced Nimrod in a brigandish sombrero hat a good deal the worse for wear, was engaged in sociable converse with Mr. Whitworth; while Mr. Christie stood by looking on, in a simple and *dégagé* costume which made a picturesque display of shirt-sleeves, jack-boots, and a huge knife stuck loosely in his belt. In the background, apparently deeply interested, were Beverley, the indoor mulatto boy, and old Lorenzo, the out-door man, an ancient negro with a fringe of white whisker and beard framing his venerable black face, and making him look exactly like a large-sized ape. To these enter Rosemary and Violet, Messrs. Conyers, Staples, Tregelva, and Harrington. John Ross's brown face beamed with a hearty smile as his audience thus suddenly and largely increased.

'Yes, sir, four splendid bucks!' he continued. 'I sold the hides and antlers to Mr. Galbraith.'

'He'll send them home as trophies of his own killing,' was Tregelva's comment.

'See here, sir!' said the hunter, lifting up a fine saddle, 'fifteen cents a pound.'

'I used to get it for two cents a pound in Colorado,' Whitworth rejoined.

'Colorado isn't Florida,' John Ross answered veraciously, and none could contradict him.

'I say, Staples,' observed Tregelva aside, 'you might try Ross with your boots. He's a big strong fellow, and he might be able to bear them.'

Whether this suggestion was advanced in jest or earnest, Mr. Staples accepted it seriously; he hastened into the house, and presently returned bearing a pair of enormous thick-soled top-boots. John Ross's genial smile spread from ear to ear as Staples approached him, boots in hand, and proceeded gravely to inquire what he thought them worth, and whether he would be inclined to enter into negotiations with a view to becoming their possessor? John Ross inspected them, weighed them leisurely and deliberately, shifting them from hand to hand, and then pronounced his opinion.

'Well, they're wuth ten or twelve dollars, but if they wuz mine I'd give ten dollars to be out of them!'

Christie, delighted at this, burst into one of

those hearty explosions of laughter by which
the new arrivals had already learned to charac-
terise him.   His unbridled mirth attracted
attention to himself and his costume.

'That's a Hyde Park turn-out, Christie,'
remarked Tregelva.

'I was admiring it,' said Rosemary, smiling;
and indeed young Christie—tall and young,
strong and lithe—had never looked handsomer
nor manlier than in his *négligé* toilet.   'And
this,' she added, delicately indicating the knife
in his belt, ' this gives a genuine frontier air  to
the costume.'

'He might go to a fancy ball as a pioneer,
mightn't he?' observed Staples, who stood  by,
still bearing his boots unabashed.

'Wouldn't you like to see him in the park,
vehicle, steed, and all?' said Tregelva, pointing to the neat 'Macy wagon,' the pride of
Christie's heart, painted a beautiful bright green

picked out with scarlet, to which he had been
harnessing a half-broken rough Texan pony
when the *fainéant* party from the piazza
swarmed into the courtyard.

'I was warm, and I took my coat off
for driving in the sun,' said Christie apologetically.

'I took off *my* coat driving one warm day,'
observed Tregelva narratively. 'I was going
to pay a visit, too, and I hung my coat
over the back of the buggy. When I got
there——'

'"The cupboard was bare,"' quoted Violet
laughingly.

'Yes, the buggy was bare. I turned round
to get my coat, and it was gone.'

'Visiting-costume *à la mode de Florida*,'
remarked Rosemary.

'Did you ever see your coat again?' asked
Violet.

'Yes; it was picked up on the road and brought back to me.'

'They're very honest about here,' put in Mr. Whitworth. 'We never lock a door nor bar a shutter.'

Here Mrs. Whitworth appeared, looking the model of a comely housewife, with a large apron tied over her dress, both her hands occupied in bearing aloft a huge citron and a dangling yard-measure.

'Look here, all of you!' she exclaimed, triumphantly displaying these trophies, 'did you ever see a finer citron? It's from the East Grove. Just measure it! Eighteen inches from eye to stem! Isn't it the prize citron of the season?'

The hunter was holding up a haunch of venison for inspection; Staples was still contemplating his rejected boots. Tregelva glanced from them to the 'prize citron,' and remarked languidly—

'Looks like market-day, or a stall at the Florida Exhibition, everybody showing off their goods!'

## CHAPTER VI.

### HALCYON HOURS.

THE day had worn on to sunset. Violet was sitting on the fallen trunk of a pine-tree on the brink of the South Lake, so called by the inmates of West Grove House. Its proper name was Lake Julia. Most of the lakes about this neighbourhood appeared to have been christened by men after their wives and sweethearts, so many were the feminine names represented in the list, from Eulalie and Virginia down to 'Sue'—not even Susan, but simple familiar Sue, while one of the fairest lakes answered to the name of Mary Jane. In favour of these and similar equally homely

designations, the aboriginal names, with their
quaint and curious euphony, have been neglected in too many places, although still a
glance at the map of Florida relieves us by
showing in how many other localities the old
Indian words, waifs and strays of the language
of a race that is rapidly passing away, are
retained.    In contrast with the appellations of
Jones and Jackson, Smith and Butler, and their
respective wives, sweethearts, and daughters,
how refreshing it is to come upon the good old
aboriginal names of Woyohokalpa, Yallaha,
Tohopekaliga, and Tallahassee! while as to
Itsopogayoxee and Okeehumkee they are a
perfect treat to roll under the tongue!   The
residents at West Grove had a little nomencla-
ture of their own ; they had always dubbed
Lake Julia 'South Lake,' in reference to the
quarter in which it lay with regard to the
house ; and they called Lake Margaret 'Silver

Lake,' from its purity and brightness, but left Lake Annabel and Lake Rosalie to flourish under their rightful titles.

On the shore, then, of the Southern Lake Julia, Violet was sitting, for a wonder, all alone. Rosemary had gone for a drive with Messrs. Conyers, Harrington, and Whitworth—the last-named was taking the two former to inspect a splendid young grove which had been placed in his hands for sale, and had invited Rosemary to occupy the fourth place in the carriage. Mrs. Whitworth was busy in the kitchen, assisting and directing Pinkie, the mulatto cook, in the preparation of guava marmalade, and Violet had taken a novel and gone down to sit by the lake.

But the novel lay in her lap neglected in favour of the sunset, and wisely so. For if her lines in life should lead her—as they at present promised to do—back to her own Northern

clime, she would have many and many an
opportunity of reading the best novels, of this
or any other day, for one chance of contemplating such a sunset as this.

The whole west was one scarlet fire, which
shaded by undefinable degrees into the purest
of pellucid blue above ; towards the east those
dream-like depths of azure melted into a soft,
dull, pink haze, which hung like a filmy roseate
veil over all the eastern half of the heavens.  In
the crystal-clear bosom of the lake every vary-
ing tint of the sky, every leaf and branch of
the tall stirless pine-trees, the green luxuriant
tangle of underwood on the banks, was mirrored.
The living landscape was not more purely,
clearly distinct, in detail of line and colouring,
than its reflection below the glassy surface of
the lake.  Only at the edge ' the water washing
in the reeds ' faintly broke the silence.  Violet,
keenly alive to all that was beautiful in life

and in nature, the sense of beauty thrilling softly through her every nerve, sat wrapt in dreamy content.

Presently on the far side of the lake a streak seemed to separate itself from the bank. The streak was shooting out into the water, crossing the lake; it developed into a boat—a boat rowed by one man, who was heading his course towards the spot where she sat. Violet, well content before, felt a sense of fuller contentment still as she recognised that the oarsman was Max Randolph, whistling softly as he pulled across the placid lake, his gun lying on the thwarts.

She did not rise up to greet so old a friend, but looked up and smiled as he grounded his boat and sprang ashore. She had not seen Max Randolph alone since the prolonged *tête-à-tête* of their journey from New York, and she was not sorry to find this offered opportunity of one of the old quiet talks with this good friend and comrade now.

'Why, where's Miss Rosemary?' he inquired. 'I thought you two were like twin cherries on one stem—Hermia and Helena business——'

'Hermia and Helena quarrelled, which we don't mean to do,' replied Violet.

'They clashed about a man,' he observed.

'Which I hope *we* shall not!' she said. 'For one thing, no man ever admires us both.'

'No,' he admitted. 'You are opposite poles. It would be very difficult to admire you both.'

He paused a minute or two, regarding her deliberately and thoughtfully, before he added, 'But there are some men who are born to achieve difficult tasks.'

'You had better try what you can achieve,' she rejoined laughingly.

'In that line? Yes,' he answered meditatively, pulling at his mustache, as is the way
of man when man is reflecting gravely,' 'I might
try! Pity Miss Rosemary isn't here, that I
might have a chance of beginning now.'

'You must try to be content for a little
while without her. Are you going up to the
house?'

'I'm in no hurry,' he replied. 'Come for
a turn in my boat, Miss Violet; it's the
pleasantest hour of the day on the water.'

Violet neither felt nor feigned any hesita-
tion. She knew it was indeed the pleasantest
hour of all the day, and, fair as was the scene
on shore, it would look fairer still from the
water.

She stepped willingly into the boat, took
her seat in the stern, and Max pushed off.

The water lapped softly against the sides of
the boat; the oars broke up the motionless

reflection of the rose and azure sky into opaline ripples, and sent tremulous wrinkles across the graceful images of the tall slim pine-trees that pointed downwards in the transparent depths. Not a sound, not even the note of a bird, broke the silence; not a cloud drifted across the pellucid sky; nothing marred the pure and perfect serenity of the hour and place.

'How lovely it is!' Violet breathed with a soft sigh of content.

'Now what did you want to bring that book out with you for?' asked Max, pointing to the volume she kept still in her hand.

'Don't abuse my book. It's a nice book; I am enjoying it very much.'

'I didn't abuse it: I only asked what you wanted with it. You were not reading it when I landed?'

'No, of course not: I was looking at you!' she laughed.

' If it's a good book you might lend it to me. I have read all my books and I want something to read.'

' You won't care about this,' she said ; ' it is a love-story.'

' I don't care much about love-stories generally,' he acknowledged. ' They always seem to me a good deal of fuss about nothing.'

' A fair description of some love-stories, certainly,' she agreed.

' People make too much of love,' he observed coolly. ' It's just the gilt on the ginger-bread.'

' Not the staff of life itself? ' she rejoined smiling.

' No ; just a bit of gilding, easily rubbed off, put on to please children—and fools. Heartless view, isn't it ? Shocks you, doesn't it ? '

' Well, even if your view is the right one,' she said, forbearing to pronounce sentence on

the said view, 'wouldn't you rather have your
ginger-bread gilt than not?'

'I don't know,' he replied ; 'gilding's un-
wholesome. Perhaps it's a case of sour grapes,'
he added ; 'I never have had my ginger-bread
gilt.'

'Isn't that your own doing?'

'I suppose it is,' he said ; 'but if nature left
a heart out of my anatomy, is that my fault?
I wish I *could* be in love! Wonder how it
would feel to be like that poor young
Fletcher?' naming a love-lorn swain whose
piteous case had been a subject of observation
and comment to them both. 'I wouldn't mind
trying it for an hour, just for a new sensation!'

'Have you never been in love, then?'
Violet asked him frankly, lightly, but with a
little real curiosity underlying the lightness of
her tone.

'I?' He laughed his short sneering laugh. 'Not in my line at all to make a fool of myself —in that way, I mean. There are plenty of other ways left.'

'There are, indeed,' she said, 'and worse ways too.'

'I don't know about worse ways,' he demurred. 'The worst mischief in the world is always made by women. No man ever got into any serious trouble yet that a woman wasn't at the bottom of it.'

'We might just as fairly and truly reverse the case,' she replied spiritedly. 'Transpose the pronouns and read man for woman.'

'Women feel less,' asserted Max dogmatically with a certain doggedness of air which he generally assumed when he was saying what he didn't mean.

'Less than you, who don't feel at all?' she retorted.

'Because Dame Nature was kind enough to give me a good tough piece of india-rubber in place of a heart it doesn't follow that other fellows are as lucky. Some of them come to awful grief. But one can't be very sorry for a man who makes a fool of himself about a woman. He shouldn't let himself be fooled.'

'I sympathise more with the fool than the wise man,' she observed.

'Naturally, as you profit by his folly.'

'And sometimes share it,' she suggested.

'And get off the easiest,' he said.

'No, that we don't!' she replied; 'a woman always comes off the worst.'

'Who blames a woman,' Max asked a little bitterly, 'for spoiling a man's life?'

'And what penalty does a man pay for wrecking a woman's life?' Violet rejoined.

'He doesn't do it,' was the answer. 'At least, not in the run of cases. I suppose you're

thinking of Mat Carew's affair with Lucy Pater-
son? I tell you, women's feelings are

As moonlight unto sunlight and as water unto wine.

The very next season Miss Lucy married some
rich banker.'

'Do you think her marrying the second
proves she didn't care for the first?' inquired
Violet.

'Comfortable for the second, according to
the view you suggest,' he remarked.

'We run on lines that will never meet,' she
said; 'we start from different premises; I am
afraid we shall never find a point at which to
meet and agree.'

'That would be sad,' he replied; 'I'm
always sorry not to agree with you, Miss
Violet.'

She looked at him steadily, questioningly,
as she inquired, 'Is that " rote sarkastic "?'

He met her frank asking gaze fully; his inscrutable grey eyes looked level into her clear blue ones, and told absolutely nothing, as he replied, ' Must every civil thing I say be ironical ? '

' When it is said to me ! ' she answered, half laughing, half in earnest.

' Am I such a bear to you ? ' he asked.

' No, no,' she protested sweetly. ' But we have never cultivated the habit of saying civil things to each other, have we?' she added, with one of her pretty confiding smiles.

' Well, no, we haven't,' he agreed. ' Do you think it's time we began?'

' We get on very well as we are,' she said lightly.

' Very well,' he assented, looking at her with his keen unsmiling gaze.

' And we won't begin to quarrel now,' she added—'not on such an evening as this, when everything is so lovely and calm and peaceful!'

'And not when you're alone in the boat with me,' he added. 'Choose a safer time. Keep the peace with me, or I might upset the boat.'

'Then you would have to swim with me to shore!'

'Oh, no—not if you abused me. In that case, I should swim ashore by myself; only, perhaps, as I'm foolishly good-natured, I might leave you an oar.'

# CHAPTER VII.

### LA REINE S'AMUSE.

THE sun has gone down in golden light behind the western woods; the lakes are turned to liquid gold; the cloudless azure of the sky deepens slowly and softly as the veil of twilight sinks over it, tenderly as sleep steals on the weary. Above the sunset, high in the west, one star trembles like a diamond dewdrop.

Most of the West Grove House party are out on the south piazza, enjoying the balmy beauty of the breezeless evening, watching the amber light of the sunset deepen into orange, and the orange glow into fiery red. They are talking about as much as usual—that is to say,

a desultory dropping fire of fragmentary conversation is going on.

' "Twinkle, twinkle, little star!"' quotes
Christie, who is the only one standing up, all
the rest of the party lounging in more or less
recumbent attitudes in rocking- or reclining-
chairs.

'What little star is it?' asks Violet.

'That's the evening star,' replies Harrington.

'It's Venus.' Staples volunteers his item
of astronomical information. 'Venus always
comes out just there over the sunset.'

'Venus winked at me,' says Tregelva languidly. 'I wish she wouldn't! I don't like it.'

'Tell her not to,' observes Violet; 'it's not
proper.'

'Are you awake, Mr. Tregelva?' asks
Rosemary. 'I was nearly asleep, and I thought
you were too.'

Rosemary, in a white dress, and with a

sultanesque air, is reclining in the hammock, of which she has lately taken exclusive possession, dislodging Staples, whose favourite lounging-place it used to be.

'Did you see Galbraith to-day?' asks Tre-gelva, proving his wakefulness by sitting a trifle straighter up. 'He's got to be a regular cracker—a three days' beard and a Panama hat, and no collar nor cuffs.'

'We're all beginning to look like crackers,' says Harrington. 'Conyers has got a regular cracker hat.'

'What's the use of wearing a Bond Street hat here?' demands Conyers.

'What *are* crackers?' inquires Violet, to whom the term conveys but a vague idea.

'Crackers are the—er—natives,' replies Tregelva.

'The real natives were Indians,' Harrington corrects him. 'Crackers are the white settlers.'

'Then if you settle here you'll all be crackers,' Violet argues logically.

'Crackers aren't gentlemen,' Conyers objects with stolid gravity.

'The're pasty-faced fellows who live in log-huts and tell the time by the sun,' observes Tregelva.

'They're the poor whites,' continues Harrington. 'They lead a primitive kind of life. If you see a fellow who looks as if he'd come out of an old-clothes shop, he's generally a cracker. I saw one the other day with a very dirty old blanket pinned round him instead of a coat.'

Staples, who is seated as usual with his head drooping forward on his breast, his hands deep in his pockets, his feet on a chair, and his knees drawn up at an acute angle, here observes narratively—

'I've sold a coat to-day to a nigger for two

pounds. It was a good coat,' he adds a little regretfully, ' but an awful bad fit.'

' Why don't you go into the " old clothes " business, Mr. Staples?' inquires Rosemary; ' you'd take to it like a young duck to the water.'

' Thank you, Miss Heath,' he replies rather resentfully, ' but I've no Hebrew blood in my veins ! '

' The blood of the Rothschilds doesn't course there,' observes Tregelva.

' Staples is such a good trader,' says Harrington maliciously, ' he'll die a millionaire.'

' No, I shan't,' Staples contradicts flatly. ' And I've traded my last. I've no more coats to sell.'

' *I* shall be reduced to part,' says Tregelva, ' if I don't hear from home soon.'

' Not got your letter yet?' asks Violet.

' No, nothing yet. If the governor won't

cash up, I shall have to stay here for the remainder of my natural life.'

They are all by this time on mutually frank and confidential terms, and are well aware that Mr. Tregelva, with no bank account of his own, depends entirely on ' the governor's' remittances from home.

' He has had to " cash up " rather often before, hasn't he ? ' suggests Rosemary from her hammock.

' Ye—yes—pretty often,' the eldest hope of the Tregelvas acknowledges placidly. ' I've made a mess of a good many things.'

' And now you are going to try just how bad a scrape you can get into with orange groves ? ' she rejoins.

' I'll back him to make a mess of everything he tries his hand at,' laughs young Harrington.

' Too bad ! ' drawls Tregelva, adding with,

if possible, a more indolent air than ever, a tone as if his eyes were just closing in slumber, 'Turn him out! Won't somebody turn him out?'

'That reminds me of an awfully good story,' eagerly begins Christie, who, whenever he gets anything good, either a joke or guavas, is always unselfishly eager for others to participate in his enjoyment. 'It was in an Irish theatre—and they were dissatisfied somehow with the orchestra—and there was a row in the gallery. One fellow was making a great disturbance, and so they were calling, "Turn him out!" "Throw him over!" when a man got up and shouted out, "Don't waste him, boys! *kill a fiddler with him!*"'

Staples and Harrington laugh; Conyers and Tregelva vouchsafe a smile; Rosemary observes sweetly—

'Oh, Mr. Christie, that story's as old as the hills!'

Staples begins a defence of Christie's powers of entertainment.

'Christie can tell some devilish——' he picks himself up and substitutes 'some very good stories.'

'Hullo, Staples!' exclaims Tregelva, 'are you going to become a reformed character?'

Staples looks rather sulkier than usual, and appears absorbed in striking a match.

'Have you heard Staples swear, Miss Preston?' Tregelva continues.

'*Does* he swear?' she inquires.

'He can—a little—when he tries.'

'I have not heard him,' she replies. 'It is a treat in store.'

'Perhaps it's not in store,' demurs Staples; 'perhaps you never will hear me.'

To do Mr. Staples justice, he did not intend that she should; but nevertheless, that very evening, in passing the smoking-room at a moment when Staples happened to have dropped and broken his favourite pipe, both Rosemary and Violet were made aware of that young man's extraordinary fluency of profane language and proficiency in devising original and ingenious oaths.

'Do you know, Vi, my dear,' said Rosemary, when the two girls were by themselves in the safe seclusion of their own room, 'I have come to the conclusion that it is a mistake to diffuse one's self too much; and that it is just what we have been doing here. We have both been diffusing ourselves too much. I believe it is a practice in warfare for the best marksmen not to fire at random, but each choose out his man and pick him off. Let us be good markswomen, Vi; let us each select an object —and pick him off!'

'They do not strike me as being, any of them, very vulnerable,' Violet observed; 'but even Achilles had his weak point, and I've no doubt you will succeed in getting *your* shaft in at your victim's heel, whoever he may be. Have you made up your mind which one to choose?'

Rosemary inclined her head a little on one side thoughtfully.

'I think I'll have a shot at Tregelva,' she mused. 'He's rather nice. He has good eyes; a pleasant voice, and a very nice soft laugh.'

'How about Max Randolph?' asked Violet lightly.

'Oh, I can run a pair!' replied Rosemary, reckless of consistency in her metaphors. 'And you, Violet, why don't you try Staples and Conyers? The ugliest and the handsomest! They'd make a good pair!'

'*I* am not sharpshooter enough to hit two at once,' Violet laughed. '*You* are like the circus-riders, Rosie, who gallop round on two horses, a foot on the back of each.'

'And get thrown sometimes,' said Rosemary drily.

'Which you won't,' rejoined Violet. 'Failure is not in your line!'

'I *have* failed,' Rosemary answered moodily. Then, hurriedly, as if averting some possible approach to a forbidden subject, she added, 'Remember old Carmichael!'

'Well, he was the exception that proves the rule,' replied Violet.

'The rule must pay for the exception,' said Rosemary, with a look in her deep dark eyes that boded no good to her victims.

'I don't think I get on with Conyers,' Violet observed confidentially the next day—having presumably made tentative and experimental endeavours to thaw that silent and statuesque Antinous into conversation. 'I can't make him talk.'

'I think it would pass mortal woman's power—even mine,' Rosemary added, with a little laugh—'to make him talk. But much may be achieved without speech.'

'Mute eloquence of the eyes?' rejoined Violet. 'I should like to see Conyers wrought up to such a pitch!'

'Perhaps you may. There's no knowing what strange sights may be in store. He's certainly good-looking.'

'He's more than good-looking,' Violet replied, with artistic and impersonal enthusiasm. 'That low broad forehead and pure Greek nose are a perfect pleasure to contemplate! Perhaps it would be too much to expect social or intellectual qualities of him as well. He is nothing but a profile!'

'Well, Vi, if you think his profile—his

" Attic forehead and his Phidian nose "—worth a little pains——'

' But I really don't,' said Violet, as Rosemary arrived at an eloquent and significant pause. ' He's not at all in my line.'

' Well, if you don't care to try him,' Rosemary rejoined musingly, ' it seems to me a pity he should be wasted.'

' " Don't waste him ! Kill a fiddler with him !" ' quoted Violet, laughing.


It is a warm, still, moonless night, but alive with stars. Large, and bright, and golden—such stars as our England never knows—they glow out from the depths of sapphire sky. The West Grove House party are as usual sitting outside enjoying the air. On one side of the great central doors—which stand wide open, of course, and from which a pale stream of lamplight pours out across the piazza—Mrs. Whitworth and Violet Preston are seated, surrounded by a little court, consisting of Tregelva, somnolent and smoking, swaying in a rocker ; Christie, wide awake and ready to laugh at the tiniest of perceptible jokes ; and Staples, drooping limply in a chair tilted on its hind legs against the wall, his chin, as usual, on his shirt-front, while his hands, being occupied with his pipe and light, happen for once to be out of his pockets.

On the other side of the bar of light, which strikes out from the hall across the piazza to the lawn, Rosemary sways in the hammock, with Max Randolph seated by her side, and Chadwick and the Fraser boys at a respectful distance. An empty chair is beside her, and near it towers the tall athletic figure of Conyers, in an attitude not so much irresolute as contemplative, with his eye on the chair.

It is a comfortable chair, and, as he meets the side-glance of Rosemary's dark eyes and Rosemary's smile, he takes his seat there.

Violet sees, without looking at, Rosemary and her surroundings—has seen for the last half-hour how mutually absorbed have Rosemary and Max Randolph been.   The conversation in Violet's own group is not enthralling, although it ought to be mildly interesting to her, whose sympathies are always so ready.

She likes Christie, and he is heart and soul absorbed in talking about a piece of land he has just bought, through Mr. Whitworth's good offices ; the admirable qualities of this land, ' lake-front, half pine, half hammock,' and his plans for house and grove, fill the boy to over-brimming.   Mrs. Whitworth much encourages his enthusiasm, silently hoping that his hearers may ' go and do likewise ' ; and Violet listens with apparent interest, and puts in an appro-

priate remark now and then. Her face is not
turned towards Rosemary and her court, but
out of the corner of her eye she takes in every
detail of that group.

She could have been one of it if she had
liked. She could have had that chair wherein
Conyers has disposed himself. It had been
vacant some time; she could have sat there
with Rosemary and Max Randolph. They
were her two best friends and most congenial
spirits. Why had she not joined them? She
scarcely knows herself, but her attention keeps
wandering across to them, even when Tregelva,
waking up at some allusion that recalls Ascot
to his mind, (from which it and its kindred
occasions appear never to be very far-distant,)
sets off on a train of racing reminiscences. He
always dates everything by the sporting calen-
dar—'It was the year when Bras d'Or won

the Derby'; 'It was just after the Grand National,' and so on.

Violet does not take any interest in races; she does take interest in watching from the distance how Rosemary draws that laconic Antinous, Conyers, into sociability, and devotes more and more attention to him, and less and less to Max Randolph. A few fragments of the conversation float to her ears; she catches the words of Rosemary's sweet confidential murmur—

'And this little spaniel had the loveliest long ears, just like satin.'

Then Conyers evidently is wound up to the pitch of relating an anecdote, of which Violet only hears the final words—

'I sent for three vets to see it, but the poor beggar died.'

At this touching crisis Max Randolph gets up and walks away. Conyers and Rosemary pursue the line of canine reminiscences with a mutually confidential air; and Max, pulling himself up tall in the lamplight, looks round at the other members of the party, and comes across to Violet's side, but only to say 'Good-night' and explain that it is time for him to get home to Martin's.

'I saw you slaying the fiddler,' Violet said to Rosemary that night, in their confidential chat.

'Yes,' Rosemary smiled, with a satisfied air, interpreting this dark saying aright.

'Max didn't half like my talking so much to Conyers. Your Apollo isn't brilliant, Vi; but he serves his purpose.'

And Violet wondered, but did not ask, why Max should care for Rosemary's talking to Conyers, and whether he cared—much?

# CHAPTER VIII.

## THE OLD WORLD IN THE NEW.

THERE was to be a dance—a ' hop '—a reception—an entertainment—thus it was variously designated in the neighbourhood—to celebrate the opening of the great new Osceola Hotel. All the residents and visitors for miles around were invited—indeed, a general invitation was issued to all the world within reach. The inmates of West Grove House, of course, were going—at least, a select detachment of them; and the questions of the day were, which of the party were going, how they were to go, and how they were to dress. Some of the young men had brought out evening suits in their trunks, and some of the others had laughed at them for bringing dress-clothes out to the backwoods; but now the laugh was turned, and the happy possessors of the swallowtails and superfine linen of civilised evening dress were envied.

Tregelva actually had half a dozen pairs of white gloves; and as he expressed himself willing to accommodate his friends by the loan thereof, he was voted the prince of good fellows. Unfortunately, he had about the smallest hand of the whole party; and Conyers, having striven in vain to compress his digits into the limits of Tregelva's gloves, gave it up as a bad job, and magnificently avowed his intention of driving to the nearest town to buy a pair.

'I'm not going to give three dollars for gloves to wear one night,' was the sensible decision of Mr. Staples. 'I shall go without, or wear my old tan ones.'

'I've got two odd ones,' said Christie, cheerfully accommodating himself to circumstances; 'I shall wear one, and carry the other with an easy flourish.'

'I've burst a pair of Tregelva's,' observed Harrington, ' but I think a burst glove's better than none; it shows at least a recognition of civilised customs.'

The question of the division of the company in the three vehicles of which the West Grove stables could boast ran the dress question very close in the general interest. It was suggested that Conyers and Tregelva should go in the single buggy, while Christie gave Staples a lift in his Macy wagon, and the two girls accompanied Mr. and Mrs. Whitworth in the double buggy. This distribution was arranged less in the interests of the conventional proprieties of the Old World than out of consideration for the ladies' dresses, as the large double buggy was much easier to get into and out of than either of the other vehicles.

Chaperonage was an institution deemed of little importance in South Florida at this stage of its development.  The native young ladies not only dispensed with the 'chaperon,' but turned the Old World code of etiquette upside down, by themselves inviting the escorts who found favour in their eyes ; which custom, being carried out in the cases of Christie and Harrington, the two of the West Grove young men who mixed most sociably with the outer world, had the effect of causing some alteration in the proposed arrangements for the drive.

'Here !' exclaimed Christie, beaming with broad smiles, as much of amusement as of flattered vanity, 'what am I going to do?  Here are *two* girls who have written to ask me to take them to the Osceola ball !'

'Take the best-looking !' advised Conyers.

' Take 'em both,' said Tregelva.

' Toss up a coin for it—heads or tails ! ' suggested Staples.

' I've got an invitation from a young lady too, who says she'll be glad of my escort,' said Harrington, with modest pride. ' I shall have to hire a trap.'

' Seems like the cart before the horse,' observed Staples, with sturdy conservative disapproval of innovation, ' for the girls to ask fellows to take them to a ball. They've queer ways out here.'

' It doesn't speak very well for the chivalry of the young men about the neighbourhood if the girls are reduced to *ask* for escorts,' remarked Rosemary.

' No, really it is quite the other way, Rose,' said Violet ; ' it is that the girls regard a free and unquestioned privilege of choice as one of their natural and inalienable rights.'

' Sort of leap-year business,' observed

Tregelva.   'I wonder if they carry it out to the end?'

'May we be there to see!' exclaimed Rosemary—'to see you all—the whole band and brigade of you—reluctantly borne to the altar by conquering crackers!'

'It would take a team of crackers to get *me* to the altar,' Tregelva replied, with complacent security.

'They won't try *me*,' growled Staples.

'See the dangers of popularity!' laughed Violet, turning to Christie and Harrington, the popular members of the brotherhood.

'They're just as nice, good, well-behaved girls as any others,' said Christie, always kindly and fairly disposed towards mankind in general, including women.  'It's only the difference of customs.'

'This is just a new country, and they haven't any manners or customs yet; they don't know *our* ways,' observed Harrington, with a grand air of kindly tolerance. He probably also felt his honour engaged in the justification of the young lady who had shown her good taste by her choice of him as an escort.

'I think they *have* manners of their own— at least, I'm glad they're not *ours*,' remarked Staples.

'To fail in resemblance to *our* customs is of course a grave shortcoming,' said Violet. 'But they will improve. Progress is rapid here. In a very few years this neighbourhood will be just like a suburb of New York.'

'Miss Preston says that, as if to hang on to the outskirts of New York was getting up to the top of the ladder,' said Tregelva.

'To my mind,' pronounced Conyers, 'New York is a beast of a place.'

'That settles it,' said Violet seriously. 'New York's doom is sealed.'

The important evening arrived, and, according to the altered programme, Conyers and Tregelva set off in Christie's 'Macy wagon,' Staples also accepting a lift therein, and being relegated, like a sack of goods, to the back of the wagon, where he sat on the edge, with his feet dangling, and enjoyed a healthful jolting which shook him into an even more limp and loose-jointed condition than usual. Christie, for whose convenience the exchange of vehicles had been made, took his fair charge in the single buggy, while the double one conveyed Mr. and Mrs. Whitworth, Rosemary and Violet. Harrington escorted the young lady who had honoured him by her choice in a hired buggy, and had all he could do to manage his steed—an imperfectly broken Texan pony, who started off with a bolt, and continued bolting at intervals all the way; but, fortunately, Harrington's companion, bred in a frontier life, had good strong nerves, and could probably have driven a half-broken horse as well or better than *he* could do.

It was a medley crowd that filled the parlours, the piazzas, the corridors, and swarmed up and down the stairs, of the Osceola Hotel. All the visitors and residents for miles around were there; 'all ranks and conditions of men,' from north and south and east and west, and from the other side of the 'big ferry'—an *omnium gatherum* of tourists, settlers, and of course a goodly muster of those health-seekers and fortune-seekers who begin as tourists and are as likely as not to end as settlers.

The cockney, *h*-less and complacent, was represented here; so was the English aristocrat and the New York millionaire. Hyde Park and Fifth Avenue had sent their contingent; here too was the canny Scot—the best and most thrifty and industrious of settlers; and

here his neighbour from the Emerald Isle, come
to seek under another flag the living he could
not make in his own 'most distressful country.'
Here in full force, of course, was the American.
Here were citizens, Republican and Democratic,
from every State in the Union; the Southerners,
although this region lay so far down in the
sunny South, being, oddly enough, considerably
in the minority.

Every variety of dress was to be seen, from
the correct and conventional evening toilet of
civilised society, to the cuffless, collarless
simplicity of the frontier. Violet Preston's
dress, of white nun's veiling, was simple
enough; but its very lack of adornment was
the cunning of that art which conceals art. It
was eminently becoming to her pure and
delicate beauty; and so thought every man,
while every woman of the outer world appreciated its perfect taste and style; only the

pioneer-women would probably have liked it better had it been more ornate and had a bit of colour about it; the tulip would have pleased them better than the lily.

Rosemary was in black—not sombre black, but black that was brilliant with shining jet and beads—transparent black lace revealing the snowy gleams of her fair arms and shoulders —black relieved by sprays of white flowers and delicate ferns nestling in the folds of lace and in the ruddy-golden chesnut of her hair.

There were some ladies in satin, and others in serge; one wore a resplendent white silk which looked like a bridal attire; others had morning or walking-dresses smartened up by bows of ribbon or knots of flowers. Some were 'beauty unadorned,' while some had piled on all the ornaments they could get together, regardless of the motley effect produced by the juxtaposition of amber beads and silver arrows or turquoise locket and emerald brooch.

The styles of dancing were as varied as the toilettes; some of the couples seemed to regard a waltz as an opportunity for acrobatic display, so wildly did they career down the long room.

The West Grove House party kept together of course. Max Randolph joined them; indeed, being so frequently there, he might almost be counted as one of the house party. Then the Staunton House young men came round seeking introductions to the West Grove ladies. Mr. Staunton, like Mr. Whitworth, received a select number of his young country-men to board, afforded them opportunites of studying orange-culture, and gave them the advantage of his advice and experience in the matter of purchase of the land he held for disposal. But Staunton House could boast of no such attractions as the Whitworths' two fair guests; and Mrs. Staunton was just an ordinary, elderly, busy housewife. So 'the Staunton fellows'—as Mr. Whitworth's young men called them, with a complacent sense of having the best of it—gathered round the West Grove House party assiduously; and Violet and Rosemary, already engaged a dozen dances ahead, could have had half a dozen partners each for every waltz, and really found it difficult to divide themselves fairly amongst the numerous aspirants for the pleasure of their hands for the dance.

Mrs. Whitworth also, a good-looking matron, and a good dancer, had as many partners as she could wish. Christie and Harrington danced, of course, first with their own especial charges, then handed them over to their friends and countrymen, to whom also other ladies of the neighbourhood were introduced.

A young person in a scarlet dress trimmed

with big bunches of blue artificial flowers, who had apparently put on all the trinkets pertaining to her mother and grandmother as well as her own, bore off the resigned but not too willing Staples.

Violet could not repress a smile as she saw him, palpably out of breath, flushed and panting, looking over his partner's shoulder with a pathetic expression of endurance as he was whirled around in the young lady's vigorous clasp. This trial over, he hastened to Violet's side with an air of seeking shelter under her friendly wing.

'My word!' he said, 'she talked nineteen to the dozen, and jumped half her own height in the air at every step!'

'Come, Miss Violet, there's your favourite waltz,' said Max Randolph, offering her his arm as the band struck up 'Sweet Dream Faces.'

Violet looked up in his face with her soft smiling eyes.

' I think I am promised two or three deep for this already,' she said, but not very decisively.

' If you only *think*,' he replied, ' never mind thought! Possession is nine points of the law,' and he slipped his arm round her waist with a coolly proprietary air.

' I was just going to ask you for this waltz,' said Staples in an aggrieved tone.

' Too late!' she laughed as she was whirled away.

On account of the privilege of old friendship, Max Randolph was favoured by more dances with Miss Heath and Miss Preston than any other man there—more, indeed, than the compatriots of these young ladies considered him, an alien, fairly entitled to enjoy. He spent a goodly part of the evening with Miss Preston,

but a goodlier proportion still with Miss Heath ;
indeed the ladies of the neighbourhood derived
but little benefit from Mr. Randolph's presence
at the entertainment.

Once it chanced that he and Conyers, on
their way to ask Rosemary's hand for the waltz,
arrived at their goal simultaneously, and both
at once got as far as ' Miss Heath, will you—'
before, each perceiving he had not got the start
of the other, they mutually paused.   Rosemary
looked up, with her rich dark brown eyes full
of half-mischievous and tantalising sweetness.

'Now you both want me to dance?' she
said.   'Can I be cut in two like Solomon's
baby?'

' It  wasn't  Solomon's  baby,'  objected
Conyers; 'it was the baby he was giving a
judgment about.'

'True; but, anyhow, am I to be treated
like that baby?'

'Rather than have you cut in half, I'll waive my claim,' said Randolph.

'So would I,' added Conyers, thinking it right to echo this sentiment.

Rosemary looked at the first speaker, ignoring Conyers' well-meant protestation.

'You haven't a claim to waive,' she observed, with her slow imperial smile.

'Not the claim of old friendship?' he replied.

'You might put in that claim with Violet, but scarcely with *me*,' she said in a tone too sweet to be repellent.

'Then it's "off with the old love," is it?' he rejoined quickly, prompt to accept a dismissal. Although he smiled, the smile had a mocking cast as he spoke of the 'old love,' and Rosemary fancied she caught a moment's glint of displeasure in his eye.

'No; I'll divide—not myself, but the

dance,' she said. 'And the old—friend,' with a coquettish glance and pause between the adjective and the substantive, 'shall have the first turn!'

'What is to become of you now?' she inquired when that turn was over, and, Conyers' time having come for the latter half of the dance, Max Randolph had to give her up to him.

'I think I'll ask that comely dame in green to have pity on me,' he said, glancing at a very stout and rubicund lady in a bright grass-green gown with a whole rainbow of feathers and flowers in her hair.

'Yes, it's just the colouring to please an artist's eye,' agreed Rosemary; 'and, like Fair Margaret in the ballad,

> She has kilted her robes of green
> A piece below her knee!'

It was true that the lady's dress was made

of a serviceable walking-length and exhibited
a pair of stout full-sized boots.

Notwithstanding his expressed admiration,
Mr. Randolph refrained from seeking an introduction to her, and waited for the chance of
a turn with Violet, who was then finishing a
waltz with Mr. Harrington.

A couple of dances later on, Violet and
Conyers came across Staples, with rather a
forlorn and sulky look, edging his way to
the door.

' Not dancing, Mr. Staples ? ' said Violet.

' No ; there's no one to dance with. You
and Miss Heath are always engaged ; and I've
paid my toll to the natives—they won't catch
me again ! '

' I did pity you as I saw you borne along
into the fray,' said Violet, smiling at the picture
in her mind's eye.

' She jumped more like a kangaroo than

a woman,' said Staples, his grievance still fresh and green in memory. 'And now just look at Tregelva's girl: she gets round the room in six leaps and a bound.'

'I hope the sweet consciousness of duty sustains him, but I think he'd like to pause in his wild career,' observed Violet. 'Christie's partner hops about like a parched pea, doesn't she?' she added, turning her attention to the next couple.

Staples chuckled, as if he derived some enjoyment from the contemplation of his friends' trials.

'Harrington's girl is very pretty, and quite a nice-mannered little thing too,' Violet continued.

'She's not bad, as girls go. I danced twice with her,' said Staples tolerantly.

'We are going out on the piazza, the moonlight looks so lovely,' Violet said as she and

her partner, fair handsome Conyers, handsome and taciturn as ever, passed out of the
dancing-room.

' *I'm* going to smoke,' observed Staples ; but
after standing about in an aimless hesitating
way for a moment or two, he followed in Violet's track.

On the piazza, Max Randolph and Rosemary
were seated on a bench just big enough for
two. The manner in which their heads inclined
towards each other as if by the law of natural
attraction, and the fluent murmur of under-
toned voices and low laughter, gave evidence
that they were perfectly and happily absorbed
in each other's society.

Violet and Rosemary never interfered with
each other's flirtations. When one of them
was enjoying a *tête-à-tête*, the other never, under
any temptation, intruded upon it. So Violet
and Conyers sauntered up and down and made

remarks about the moonlight. Such moonlight it was too! the full white glory of the Southern night, the whole landscape—the usual landscape of pine-trees, an orange-grove, and a lake—bathed in a pearly flood of pure light like dawn when dawn is just brightening into day.

The girls' faces were fair in the silvery beams, whose effulgence brought out every delicate line and dimple clear ; and so thought more than one of the young men who were lounging on the piazza.

Presently Rosemary glanced up at Tregelva, who was passing slowly and indolently by, and stopped him by some casual smiling remark. Seeing the *tête-à-tête* turned into a trio, Violet, the next time she passed, brought her partner to a halt ; and then Staples came up and joined the group. Max Randolph rose and offered his seat to Violet, and, as Rosemary nodded and

added her sanction to the invitation, she accepted the offer.

'I have danced the shoes off my feet!'
observed Rosemary, leaning back with a pretty
air of weariness, and looking up at the young
men as they stood round.

'Cinderella,' remarked Tregelva, languidly
and not very appropriately, and was corrected
by Conyers, who remarked with the crystalline
terseness which distinguished him—

'Cinderella only lost one shoe.'

'I've not had such a night's dancing,' continued Rosemary, 'since I came into exile!'

'Does it seem to you so much like exile
to-night?' asked Violet. 'As for me, I really
feel as if I were back in the civilised world!'

'If one could shut one's eyes to the wild
dancing of the aborigines,' rejoined Rosemary.
'I think Mr. Tregelva'—glancing at him with
a smile—'wished that he *was* back in the civi-

lised world while he was being whirled around by his cracker young lady!'

'By George!' Tregelva agreed heartily, 'I had to pull her in and take her on the curb, else she'd have had me clean off my feet!'

Max Randolph had gradually drifted round to Violet's side.

'Like old days, to-night, somehow, waltzing to these old tunes,' he observed, bending over her. 'Do you hate recalling old days?'

'Not when the old days are such pleasant ones as many we have had,' she replied.

'*We're* none of us in it if they get talking of old days,' remarked Staples, half-laughingly, half-grumblingly.

'*I'm* in it, am I not?' said Randolph, still looking at Violet. 'We have had good times on both sides of the ocean, haven't we? Miss Rosemary, won't you join in?'

'No; speak for yourselves, as far as regards

*this* side of the ocean. I left *my* good days behind in my native island, and I don't expect to find them again till I get back there.'

' Now, Rosemary,' exclaimed Violet, ' why can't you enjoy life just as much here as there ? Do you like London fogs better than American sunshine ? '

' A great deal better,' said Rosemary stoutly.

' Miss Preston's no true Briton,' observed Tregelva.

' She'll be getting naturalised and turning into an American citizen some day,' said Staples.

' Well, if she did, her adopted country would know how to appreciate her,' remarked Randolph.

' You cannot be aware of it, but do you know that *sounds* like a compliment ? ' said Violet wonderingly.

'Perhaps I had better retract it?'

'For the sake of consistency, perhaps you had.  You have not the habit of saying civil things to *me*.'

'He keeps them all for *me*,' suggested Rosemary.

'*You* appreciate them; Miss Violet would not.'

'You never give me a chance,' replied Violet, smiling up in his face.

'Other people would say civil things to you if you gave them a chance,' put in Staples, with a rather sulky and shamefaced air.

The notion of Staples saying civil things to anybody struck Violet as so funny that she laughed outright.

'Miss Preston doesn't think much of your powers of making yourself agreeable, Staples,' remarked Tregelva.

Staples did not accept the challenge; he

retired into his shell and there shut himself up, aggrieved.

Presently they all rose to go in. Violet and Rosemary linked arms and walked together, the young men trooping round them. On the top of the broad shallow steps they paused in the full flood of moonlight that streamed in between the columns of the piazza.

'Isn't the moonlight lovely?' exclaimed Violet, looking out across the day-bright grove.

'Yes, but there are some pretty things to look at besides the moonlight,' replied Max Randolph, who stood nearest to her.

The pearly beams poured on the white dress and the black—on Violet's pure pale face and Rosemary's richer and more striking beauty. Max regarded the two with an artist's satisfaction in contemplation of the beautiful; and both looked up at him—Rosemary with 'that regal indolent air of hers!' the smile that always had a mockery or a challenge in it ; Violet with her softer, simpler glance, innocent and confiding, yet not destitute of just that touch of coquetry which is second nature to a young and pretty woman—or at least to ninety-nine pretty young women out of a hundred.

' I have paid you another compliment, Miss Violet,' he observed.

' Was *I* to have a share in it ? ' she laughed.

' A fair half,' said Rosemary.

' I leave the division to you, Miss Rosemary,' he rejoined.

' We two divide things equally, don't we, Vi ?—when we divide them at all ! ' she replied —with a touch of emphasis on the qualifying final words.

When the two friends were talking over the evening *têie-à-tête* in their room, Rosemary confided to Vi—

' Max wanted me to drive back with him in

his trap; but I thought I couldn't very well do
that. As I had gone with Aunt Em's party,
she might have thought it odd if I hadn't gone
back the same way.'

Was Max, then, falling a victim? Violet
wondered. Had he entered upon that steep
inclined path down which she had seen many
a man slip, to land helpless in the quick-
sand of ignominious subjection to Rosemary's
charms, and dependence on Rosemary's caprice.
It did not seem likely, scarcely even possible.
Max Randolph always appeared to Violet the
last man to fall in love, or to centre his thoughts
and interests anywhere outside of himself. He
had large capacities for kindness, even tenderness; but of passion or emotion in him *she*
never had seen a sign.

# CHAPTER IX.

## THE OLD, OLD STORY.

VIOLET had a simple and whole-souled faith in Rosemary's all-conquering charms. Since their early girlhood she, Rosemary's only confidante, had known all Rosemary's life, and had ample grounds for her estimate of the power of Rosemary's influence over men.

I have said that both these young women had left their first love-stories behind; and here I should like to go back and pick up those two broken threads of the past, and briefly tell what those two stories were.

Violet's was a simple story, and an 'old, old story' enough. Of good family, but with her fair face for her only fortune, the girl, of course, fell in love with a young man without a penny of income save what his father chose to allow him for pocket-money so long as it pleased him. Both families naturally objected to the engagement of this impecunious young couple. Equally naturally, Romeo and Juliet soared above such coarse, commonplace, and mundane considerations; but eventually, after domestic scenes, and stolen meetings, and the usual futile fighting of youth and love against fate as represented by family and financial difficulties, the lovers had to part; and *his* family prudently shipped him off to Australia out of temptation's way. They parted, of course, in a dream of 'hopeless hope,' of lasting love that should be 'faithful unto death.'

Arthur Leslie was the first to wake to real life. His family had procured him a post in the establishment of a wealthy merchant in

Melbourne, and he evidenced his awakening by marrying his employer's daughter, who brought her bridegroom the double dower of beauty and money. And everybody said what a good thing it was for all parties concerned—good for him and good for Vi Preston too, for she never would have looked at anyone else so long as young Leslie was free, and now, so pretty as she was, she might make a good match. Violet never blamed him; she constantly averred that Arthur's course of action was only natural, he being hopeless of *her*, so many thousand miles away, and thrown into frequent association with a lovely girl who was in everything a suitable mate. And when, not a year afterwards, came the news of Arthur's death, she was glad to her inmost heart that she never had thought hardly of her poor lost love!

And as time passed on, Violet, being a mere girl in years, and of a healthy elastic temperament, began to realise that after all there was a good deal left in life, even though her love-dream was shattered—then in time to accept and familiarise herself with the idea that she should probably marry some day—marry some wealthy and respectable member of society, with whom she would not be the least in love, but to whom she would make a dutiful and exemplary wife, and whom she would cheer-fully assist in the judicious expenditure of his money—for money he must have of course ; that was a *sine qua non*. Love was buried in her Arthur's grave ; old-maidism was an unpleasing prospect, which she declined to contemplate ; there was left, then, an eligible marriage founded on decorous regard and general suitability, and this was Violet's fancy sketch of her eventual destiny. Meanwhile, being fair and young, and much admired, and liking admiration, she amused herself by flirting in an innocent superficial way that did no much harm, and on the whole she enjoyed her life.

Rosemary's experience of love had been a bitterer one than her friend's.

Mr. Heath had two daughters by his first marriage, Letice and Rosemary, there being some half-dozen years' difference in their ages. Their mother died while Rosemary was yet a child, and two years or so afterwards he married again. His elder daughter, Letice, a delicate girl of gentle and reserved disposition, always from the first got on better with their stepmother than did Rosemary, a high-spirited and, to say the truth, somewhat wilful and troublesome child, who nevertheless was Mrs. Whitworth's favourite niece and god-daughter. Thus it naturally happened that Rosemary, especially in her early girlhood, before the angles of her character and temper got rubbed down and polished, spent a good deal of her time away from home with this aunt. The Whitworths had at that time a pretty little place on the Thames, and there, one summer, on boating bent, came the handsomest and most fascinating man Rosemary had ever seen —one George Raymond.

Her girlish beauty charmed him, and he made his admiration plain. He knew her parents; indeed it was through them that he had made the acquaintance of the Whitworths. When in London, he was a frequent visitor at the Heaths'; he intimated to Rosemary that it was his constant thought of *her* that drew him to visit at her home even while she was away; the casket was dear for the sake of the jewel it was wont to hold. In due season he told his love to Rosemary in eloquent terms, and won her promise of love and faith in return. He explained to her that family matters prevented his contemplating marriage at present, but in time, in only a little time, he might follow the dictates of his heart and win and wear his jewel, and so on.

Thus it was, with a happy secret at her heart, full of hopes and dreams, that Rosemary returned to her home. She found Letice— never very strong—looking paler, and seeming more abstracted than her wont. These two sisters had not grown up with the habit of full and free confidence, partly owing to a vein of reserve in both their natures, but chiefly because of the difference in their age, Letice having grown to woman's estate, while Rosemary was still a child. But if there was not an over-confidential relationship between the sisters, there was strong affection; and Rosemary, her perception quickened by her own love, her own sweet secret, soon began to suspect that Letice had her secret too—to dream of confiding in

Letice, and receiving this dear elder sister's confidence in return.

One day, in a mood of expansion, she went so far as to confess to Letice that there was ' somebody ' she thought a great deal of, to murmur a question whether there was not a somebody in Letice's thoughts too. And Letice faltered, ' Yes—I can't tell you now, Rosemary dear, but I will tell you all about it some day—I hope very soon.' And the very day after this first approach to confidence a friend of the family had come to call, who was an old friend of George Raymond's too, and had told them, as an open secret, of George Raymond's engagement and impending marriage; how he had long been engaged to his cousin Grace Raymond, the match, indeed, having been arranged while the betrothed couple were but children, and now the wedding-day was fixed.

Rosemary, turning herself from the crimson

of maiden shame to the white wrath of faith betrayed, cast a look at her sister. Letice, more deadly white than she, was in no case to notice her little sister's emotion. She made an effort to rise from her chair, and framed some faltering excuse to get away to her own room. Rosemary, reckless of appearances, sprang up and followed. She never could bear to think of that hour—to look back and recall the interview when the two sisters learnt they had been doubly deceived, that both their hearts had been made the playthings of an hour, treated like wildflowers, to be plucked and cast aside, the happiness of both sacrificed to the gratification of one man's vanity. Rosemary at first would not believe that her lover, her George, had been Letice's lover too, bound by vows of eternal constancy to Letice as to herself, and all the while betrothed to his cousin. She caught madly at the hope that he was

somehow wronged—that Letice had misunder-
stood him—mistaken brotherly interest for
love. Yet Letice was truthful as daylight,
and the very soul of maiden modesty and
delicacy. No! Rosemary, struggle as she
would between her faith in her sister and her
lover, could not doubt long where the truth
lay.

   Her young passionate heart was strong,
and rose armed in fiery wrath and indignation
against the man who had wronged them both.
But Letice, of a softer mould, and physically
weaker too, sank beneath the blow. The shock
of the sudden discovery of her lover's double
perfidy simply killed her. Heart-disease the
doctors called it; but that tender heart, weak
though it was, might have beat on for years
had it not been for the fatal hour that wrecked
her love and sank her life with it.

   After that scene of cruel disclosure, Rosemary had to lift her fainting sister in her strong young arms and carry her to the bed she never left again. And as she sat by her sister, dying and dead, as she realised what this one man's holiday pastime had done to them both, in Rosemary's heart the love was turned to fiery hate, the milk of tenderness and trust and faith in human nature curdled to gall. Never again did the fresh sanguine spring of youth and hope and love rise in her; it was poisoned at its source.

Her bitter brooding resentment of her sister's wrong and her own soon took the shape of desire to avenge it on the sex of the wronger. Her wounded pride was only to be soothed by fresh conquest. Love was slain by one cruel stab; the only balm was the proof of power. Rosemary, when she put aside the mourning she wore for Letice, went out into the world with one purpose—to make the most of her uncommon beauty to subjugate mankind; and as years passed on, and her girlish loveliness bloomed into splendid womanhood, her vanity waxed as the anguish of recollection waned, and full-fed vanity and bitter memories all alike urged her on the way she had chosen.

She laid herself out to win admiration, love —to lure men's hearts into her hand, that she might treat them as George Raymond had treated hers and Letice's. More than once she had tempted men away from their plighted troth and honour, won them, not to keep, but to gratify her thirst of power in the winning, to hold for a day and then fling them back disdainfully to their old loves. Over and over again she had conquered by the magic of her dark eyes, her deep sweet thrilling voice; and the pleasure of conquest had never yet palled on her. Like Violet, her programme included the conventional 'settlement in life.' She meant to marry some day when she found a really brilliant opportunity. Meanwhile it was a case of 'la reine s'amuse.'

More than once had it happened that the victims of Rosemary's ruthless 'amusement' had confided their griefs and grievances to her friend Vi Preston. She had seen men's faces pale and haggard, and boys' eyes dim for Rosemary's sake, and thus,

> Because things seen are mightier than things heard,

she who had witnessed the effects of Rosemary's conquests had a profound belief in Rosemary's power, and an equal faith in Rosemary's promise that she would 'let alone' any man whom Violet asked her for her sake to spare. It must be confessed that Rosemary was just a little vain; yet not any more self-confident than circumstances warranted her in being.

Never yet had Rosemary interfered with any of Violet's admirers, and never yet had any man placed these two in the position of rivals.

Rosemary had twice, but only twice, failed in vanquishing where she had set her face for the victory; and thus there was reason for the confidence, which Violet implicitly shared with her, that she could win any one or more of the West Grove House party whom she cared to win. But Rosemary did not seem inclined just at present to concentrate herself with a view to the undoing of any particular and especial victim. Probably, as she herself had observed, regarding the aim and object of woman's life as the conquest of man, it was a mistake to 'diffuse one's self' too much; but nevertheless she continued to diffuse herself in a general distribution of her smiles, or rather, she shifted and turned their light from one to another as her changeful moods and fancies varied.

'We may just as well enjoy the season, my Violet,' she said. 'There's nobody here eligible enough to think of *marrying*, as Aunt Em has kindly made us aware. But "unto the day, the day!" and we may as well amuse our-selves.'

So the days slipped sunnily by, and the two friends amused themselves, and not much harm was done; and day after day Max Randolph rowed across the lake in Martin's boat, or drove round the lake in Martin's buggy. Sometimes he brought Mr. Martin with him, but generally he came alone, as Martin had his own business to attend to by day, his own friends to look up in the evening, and was somewhat shy of ladies' society; which certainly could not be said of his friend and 'boarder' Mr. Randolph, who almost every fine day set up his easel and sketch-block in various parts of the Whitworths' grounds, made sketches of West Grove House from different points of view; and drew what artistic inspiration he could from the orange-groves.

It must be confessed, even by those who most highly appreciate the beauty of the orange-tree—with its snowy blossoms, and red-gold fruit, and rich smooth foliage of deep and glossy green—that the carefully cultivated model groves of these beautiful trees, pruned and trimmed and planted out in level and intermin-able straight rows at regular distances in plains of bare dead-white sand, have a monotonous effect. The unbroken symmetry of these rect-angular ranks has little indeed of the picturesque to recommend it to the artist's eye. However, there are satisfactory Florida sketches to be made of the fair lakes and the graceful pine-trees, and there is always the wild picturesqueness of the 'hammock-land' to fall back upon, always the beautiful effects of the Southern sunsets and twilights and moonrises to study : so Max Randolph, even professionally, did not fare amiss; and socially, with the free run of the West Grove House, he had certainly as ' good a time,' as he and his compatriots put it, as he could have desired. Figures were not in his line, except as touches of colour and of interest introduced into a landscape ; but he won Mrs. Whitworth's heart by painting and presenting to her a little water-colour picture of her Happy Family party assembled on the piazza ; he also portrayed Rosemary and Violet in the foreground of a characteristic Floridian scene of palm and pine and lake. He kept this little study for himself, although both of them would have been pleased to accept it had he offered it.

So far as his relations with these two girls

went, matters remained very much in the same position as on their first arrival at West Grove House.

If anything, he and Violet were even more friendly than ever, more sympathetic, under the surface of the mimic warfare they often playfully carried on, more and more contented in each other's society when they chanced to be thrown together without other companions—though indeed this very seldom happened now : and, if anything, he and Rosemary flirted rather more than less than of old ; they sometimes played at being lovers, sometimes played being enemies, but never succeeded even in playing at being fraternal friends.

Rosemary made no much difference between Max Randolph and the rest of the men there; he was simply 'one of them' to her—one whom she had known a little longer, that was all. She appeared to realise no essentially different quality and material in him; and this seemed strange to Violet, to whom it was as clear as daylight that there was no one like Max. There might be many handsomer than he was, cleverer than he, better than he; but no one quite like him.

# CHAPTER X.

### THE HAPPY FAMILY.

ROSEMARY proved wonderfully successful in drawing out that taciturn Antinous, Conyers, who resembled the proverbial ' good boy ' in that he was generally seen and not heard. She also got on very well with Tregelva. Both these two graciously allowed themselves to be amused by Miss Heath's conversation, while Staples proved more amenable to the gentle influence of Violet, who took him in hand with a view to the improvement of his manners and bearing, which was certainly desirable. He did not resent her rallying him on his slouching gait, his poked head, and deeply pocketed hands.

'Could you not get your shoulders a *little* higher, and your chin a little lower?' she asked him playfully; and he showed no sign of being aggrieved or offended by the undisguised twinkle of gentle humour in her soft Irish eyes.

'I was afraid you would catch cold in church to-day, Mr. Staples,' she observed one day sweetly and seriously.

'Why?' he inquired, flattered by her apparent interest.

'You took your hands out of your pockets about the middle of the service, and I thought they would get chilblains from the unaccustomed exposure. Still, perhaps it was better late than never. Do you go to your parish church at home with your hands kept warm that way?'

'Were they in my pockets to-day?' he asked simply. 'I forgot. One forgets everything here.'

' Yes, even one's manners!' she smiled.

' You see,' he continued placidly, ' there isn't anything to think of.'

' Yes, there is : there's oranges,' she corrected him.

' I think there's more to be done with *lemons*,' he said seriously. ' These fellows are all like sheep—going one after another; they've all got oranges on the brain. Now, if I could see a place that suited me——'

' Which you will readily find, of course, by lying in a rocking-chair smoking all day, and never stirring outside the grounds!'

' I was out on Lake Rosalie yesterday.'

' Yes, asleep in the bow of the boat.'

' I beg your pardon, Miss Preston,' he rejoined, with unusual politeness and a somewhat sulky air, ' I was *not* asleep : I caught that perch you had for breakfast.'

' In a waking moment. A good perch it

was too. Well, but I interrupted you when you were just going to tell me what you would do if you saw a place that suited you?'

' I'd go in for lemons—I think lemons would pay well; and I'd put in a good piece of ground for tomatoes. But I don't see, Miss Preston, how *you* can care a straw about lemons and tomatoes and crops; you don't belong here, in this life.'

'I am always interested in the life I find myself living, even if it's only for a season.'

' *I'm* not!' he replied. 'I hate it all—at least I did when first I came. I don't find it quite so bad now.'

Mr. Staples' crass and unabashed ignorance of all things that did not come within the narrow circle of his own individual interests amused even more than it surprised Violet. His attitude frequently—but not always, as she now began to find out—was one of bored indifference and frank ignorance as to all creation outside his own personal concerns. And, so far as the indifference at least, he was rivalled by Tregelva and Conyers, who spent their time chiefly in smoking in the sunshine and the moonlight, 'dodging' the sun from the south piazza to the west piazza, and anon to the east, when the glare of the sinking sun bathed the west side in its light. Sometimes they mustered their energies to take a row on one of the lakes, and sometimes even to go a-fishing, at that loveliest hour of the day when the sun has set in glory but daylight still fills the sky, when the fish 'bite' best and give least trouble to the fisher. Occasionally they rode or drove to the nearest town, although there seemed to be nothing much to do when they got there except to visit the 'bar,' where very bad whiskey might be procured at a very high price, and ride or drive back again.

Staples, with all his peculiarities and brus-
querie, was Violet's favourite of these three;
although she admitted Tregelva to a degree of
favour he had not enjoyed before one day when
she found him and Staples ministering to the
hurts of a puppy, whose paw had been bitten
by one of the bigger dogs. They were on their
knees beside a tub, Staples carefully holding
the pup, while Tregelva bathed the wounded
paw. One of Tregelva's favourite costumes,
which he apparently deemed especially suitable
to Florida life, was a sporting-looking coat and
snowy white nether-garments. He was clad in
these to-day; and Violet observed, with a
smile, that he was shielding their spotless snow
from contact with the ground by kneeling on a
newspaper the while he tenderly bathed the
puppy's paw.

From that day Violet made up her mind
that Tregelva was a good fellow, because he

was kind to and fond of animals. Nor did she dislike the handsome, silent, statuesque Conyers, about whom there was a kind of indolent and unconscious selfishness which rather amused than annoyed her. Indeed, she managed to derive a good deal of entertainment from the contemplation of the *blasé* and nonchalant ways of this trio, to whom the *dolce far niente* appeared to be the supreme good in life.

Max Randolph also got on very well with them; and Mr. Staples condescended one day to express a favourable, albeit qualified, opinion of him.

'Randolph's a decent sort of fellow—rather a good sort for an American. I hate Yankees generally.'

'So do I,' agreed Tregelva.

'Do you know many?' asked Violet.

'No,' replied Staples, 'I don't know any

except this Randolph, and that pig of a Collins
—Ezra D. Collins—over at Wekiva.'

'I don't know any either,' said Tregelva,
'and don't want to. Don't think I ever spoke
to any.'

'How did you manage to get here then?'
inquired Violet. 'Crossing the ocean and
coming down from New York, did you travel
locked up in a trunk, or in an iron mask?'

'There were some English fellows on board,'
Tregelva replied, 'and I talked to them. Yes,
by the way,' he added, a shade of interested
reminiscence quickening his wonted lazy drawl,
'I did make acquaintance with a Yankee once;
he looked rather like a gentleman, and I got
talking to him—I smoked a cigar with him. I
thought he seemed a—an intelligent sort of
fellow. He wasn't bad form on the whole—and,
by Jove!'—with an air of indolent disgust—
'he turned out to be an infernal bagman!'

'I don't like any Yankee I ever saw, except Randolph,' said Staples, sticking to his point.

'He would not recognise himself under that denomination,' observed Violet. 'Mr. Randolph is of a Southern family—born and bred in the South.'

'Does that make any difference?' asked Staples.

'Just this,' she replied, with some warmth of protest, 'that Southerners are no more Yankees than we are. *Didn't* you know *that*, Mr. Staples?'

'No. How should I understand about these fellows and their differences? I know,' he added, anxious to display his one item of knowledge, 'that the Southerners wanted to keep their niggers slaves.'

'You do know *that?* Well, then, now know also that neither Southerners nor Western men are Yankees. The term *Yankee* only applies to the inhabitants of the six New England

States—Vermont, Massachusetts, Rhode Island,
Maine, New Hampshire, and Connecticut.'

'I wish you'd teach me a little more, Miss
Preston,' said Staples. 'I'd like being taught
by you.'

'Go home, Staples!' remonstrated Tregelva.
'You're getting too polite. Your own dog
wouldn't know you!'

'I think Mr. Staples' compliments are
ironical,' remarked Violet.

'No, they are not—I don't take the trouble
to be ironical,' he rejoined.

'You do not take much trouble about anything in life, certainly, any of you three!' she
observed.

Young Christie was a great contrast to this
*fainéant* trio—Christie, with his boyish enjoyment of life, amused and interested in everything, riding to and from his prized 'ten-
acre lot' of 'wild land,' returning tired at

evening from a hard day's work at the clearing thereof, sunburnt, flushed, and weary, but ever full of schemes and of dreams of the gold to be picked up from this ' Tom Tiddler's Ground.'

The Fraser boys had also delighted Mr. Whitworth's heart by buying; they had got a large tract of wild pine-land at a bargain, with the advantage of a lake-frontage too. The lake languished under the title of ' Red Bug ' at present, but the Frasers, who had spent several happy vacations in the English lake country, intended to call it ' Windermere.' They had already cleared a small plot in the middle of their wood, and run up a rough wooden cottage, and were every day hard at work in the carpenter's shed in the West Grove courtyard making their own furniture. These, as Mr. Whitworth was wont to say, approvingly and truthfully—THESE were the boys to get on in Florida! — these cheery, healthy, energetic young fellows, stout of heart and hand, who would plant and prune the tree, dig the ground, and chop the wood, and willingly wield

> A spade, a rake, a hoe,
> A pick-axe, or a bill!

—whichever the occasion might demand.

Harrington was always amiably willing to go about looking at land; he rode and drove miles to the north and south and east and west to inspect groves that were for sale; but, to Mr. Whitworth's despair, nothing that he saw—and every tempting kind of bargain was shown to him—pleased him sufficiently for him to write home a decisively favourable account of it to his guardians, with an application for the purchase-money. He drove about with Mr. Whitworth in the buggy; he hired a horse and made equestrian excursions, and was in so far a satisfactory inmate of the house that he gave no trouble, paid his board punctually, and occasionally vouchsafed to go a-fishing and bring in some piscatory delicacy for the table.

As to Chadwick and Spencer, they devoted their whole hearts to sport. Little did they care what tracts of high rolling pine-land could be had for ten dollars an acre, what desirable town lots were offered at a tempting bargain (generally in an unbuilt town), what beautifully laid-out groves of seedlings lay smiling, promising, at the purchaser's hand, while they could sally forth on the warpath, armed with gun and rod, net and knife—while earth and air and water teemed with living things for them to kill. Their idea of enjoying an exquisite morning of blue heavens and balmy breezes—a sunset hour of golden skies and soft and stirless air—was to go forth and slay something!

The table at West Grove House owed a great deal to their sporting proclivities. To these enthusiasts were due the breakfast dishes of black bass (locally known as trout), and of delicate perch, the turtle-soup which graced the board at dinner, the suppers of broiled quail or wild-pigeon—which the inhabitants insisted on calling 'doves,' to Violet's extreme disapprobation.

'Fancy eating *dove!*' she said. 'I believe they would eat love-birds! And to my mind it spoils the flavour of soup to be informed that the turtle was walking about on the shore of Lake Rosalie yesterday afternoon, and "Chadwick put a bullet through its head at sixty yards."'

'Well, it was a splendid shot,' observed Rosemary.

The views of these young sportsmen were not so narrow as to be confined to providing the table with fresh viands. They were just as pleased at landing a huge and hideous garpike—the devouring tiger of the waters, whose repulsive head, with its terrible teeth, they cut off and preserved as an ornament to the smoking-room—as when they brought home in triumph a fifteen-pound trout, which was exhibited on the lawn in solemn jubilee to an admiring conclave before it was conveyed in procession to the kitchen. They shot black squirrels and brown, drab squirrels and grey, some of which were experimentally made into pies, and turned out very palatable. Their especial delight, however, was to get a shot at an alligator, though this unsatisfactory and disobliging saurian generally sank when shot at, disappeared in the depths, and left the marksmen to a lively argument on the question whether he was hit or not. But, damaged or undamaged, the wise reptile seldom rose again.

They killed birds enough to fill an aviary every week, and devoted what little leisure-time they had to skinning, stuffing, and mounting their spoils. They presented the birds of brightest plumage to the ladies for their hats ; Rosemary had a blue jay in one hat, a cardinal bird in another ; Mrs. Whitworth mounted a yellow woodpecker's wing ; and even Violet, although disapproving of this wholesale slaughter of the innocents, could not say nay to a rice-bird, with its plumage like softest black velvet, and its fiery red under-wings, which Chadwick proudly presented to her. Violet by this time had thoroughly entered into South Florida life ; she conversed glibly of seedlings and budded trees, of the risks of lemons and guavas, so easily damaged or killed by the occasional frosts that swoop down from the north even upon these sunny lands of the great 'orange belt' of South Florida. She was learned on the subject of lake protection, and quite won Mr. Whitworth's heart when he heard her dilating to Harrington on the advant-

ages of the south side of a lake, whereof the
expanse of water tempers the north wind to
the seedling orange. She spoke respectfully
and appreciatively of 'high hammock' and
'rolling pine-lands,' and with a properly dis-
paraging tone of 'scrub' and 'flat' woods.'

She had discovered how far the average
Briton overestimates the necessity of broiled
chops, roast mutton, and fresh milk, of pave-
ments and made roads, inasmuch as they found
life not not only livable but enjoyable without
any of these luxuries of an effete civilisation.
Beef, poultry, fish, and venison proved sufficient
to keep the table well and variously supplied,
and Swiss milk did very well in their coffee,
while the railway line a little distance off was
good walking, and served for a constitutional
promenade quite as well as a macadamised
road, and much better than the deep, loose,
heavy sand of Florida paths. She grew quite

used to lying back reading a novel in a leak-
ing boat while Staples or Christie baled the
water out every now and then with a tin pail.
She resigned herself trustfully to driving
through pathless woods in a light buggy that
leapt and plunged over bush and over briar, flew
over fallen trees, and shaved standing stumps
as it dashed and crashed through the underwood; she learnt to regard these experiences as
rather amusing than alarming, even when the
traces slipped off the bar and the harness came
to pieces, as it very often did. There was not
much of it to come to pieces, that was one
comfort, the process of attaching a Florida
steed to his vehicle being a simple one; and if
the buggy did break down occasionally, there
had never been any damage done to any of the
party yet by these little mishaps.

Violet still enjoyed pulling oranges fresh
from the bough, and going to a tree only a few

yards from the piazza to pick a couple of
lemons when she and Rosemary had a mind for
a little social lemonade.   Nor did the delights
of fresh-plucked guavas pall upon her, and she
mourned sincerely when the cruel frost, coming
unexpectedly one night, nipped in the bud the
fair unfolding promise of Mr. Whitworth's
cherished seedling bananas.

Rosemary looked on at her friend's interest
and enjoyment in this 'level of every day's most
quiet' life with a sort of half-envious, half-
cynical tenderness.  *She* did not care one jot
for the groves and their prospects, the 'lots'
and their prices.

'I'm sick to death of it all by this time,'
she said; 'I got fairly wearied out with it at
Pine Ridge.   You are a happy girl, Vi, not to
get bored; but if you'd been as long in exile at
that wretched Pine Ridge as I have you'd hate
the very name of Florida as I do.   Oh for

London ! Oh for New York ! Oh for bricks and mortar ! ' she sighed.

But Rosemary, without taking the trouble to feign an interest in the pursuits of the place, made herself universally agreeable, and was of course an object of much admiration in the little colony ; while, for her part, although she did not like the primitive simplicity of the life, she could not be wholly discontented, with such a regiment of men, and young men, and most of them fairly well-looking men, around her.

' Let us find out all their christian-names, Vi,' she suggested one day. ' It's like living in a boys' school, hearing nothing but sur-names.'

' You couldn't call them by their christian-names if you knew them,' remonstrated Violet.

Rosemary laughed.

' I should like to address Tregelva by some

tender diminutive. He looks like a *Bertie*. I should like to call him Bertie.'

'Conyers ought to be a *Hugh*,' observed Violet; 'there always seems to be a sort of stolid solidity about Hugh.'

'And what ought Staples to be?'

'Staples? Oh, he can't be anything more romantic than a *Joe!*' laughed Violet.

However, when Rosemary put in practice her idea of asking the christian-names of the household brigade, it turned out that Mr. Staples had a legitimate baptismal right to the well-sounding prenomen of Archibald St. Julian, while the classic-featured Antinous was simple James, and Tregelva answered to the unaristocratic appellation of Thomas. Young Chadwick was Cecil Vivian, Harrington was Theodore, and Christie was Richard, but to his family always and only known as 'Dick,' which, both the girls agreed, suited him to a nicety.

# CHAPTER XI.

## IN ARCADIA.

It was a rare sunset one evening, when the usual piazza party—to wit, Messrs. Tregelva, Conyers, and Staples, Violet and Rosemary— were lounging in their accustomed places. Often and often they had enjoyed the contemplation of clear and cloudless sunsets—seas of scarlet light washing over the whole west; but seldom had they seen such stormy glory as lit up the sky this evening. Piles and piles of gorgeous golden clouds loomed up into the azure like mountains of light, filling the whole hemisphere with wild and tempestuous splendour of colour—lurid yellow blaze dashed with

purple shadow, shining slopes and peaks strug-
gling to climb up above lowering wreaths of
night-black cloud, while through the pine-trees
the mirror-clear lake seemed turned to molten
gold.

Rosemary began singing softly an im-
promptu parody on 'The Three Fishers.'

> 'Three loafers sat gazing out into the west!'

'Why three, Miss Heath?' asked Staples;
'why don't you say five? Aren't you and Miss
Preston loafing too?'

'Ladies don't loaf, Staples,' said Tregelva
reprovingly. 'They repose!'

> 'Out into the west as the sun went down,'

Rosemary continued in her sweet contralto tones.

> 'Each thought on the woman who loved him the best.'

'I can't get any further,' she observed, indolently dropping her song.

'No,' said Tregelva. 'Let's stop at the

women who love us the best! It's a very good place to stop at.'

'Where are they?' demanded Rosemary.

'Who are they?' asked Conyers.

'The girls we've left behind us!' Tregelva quoted in reply.

'Poor girls!' said Violet compassionately 'How sad they must be feeling!'

'Perhaps they have found someone else, or several somebody elses, to dry their tears,' suggested Rosemary.

'I bet they have,' growled Staples.

'Go ye and do likewise,' Rosemary observed demurely.

'Good advice!' said Tregelva. 'Quand on n'a pas ce qu'on aime, il faut aimer ce qu'on a!'

Tregelva's French accent was not bad for a true-blue Briton.

'What does that mean?' inquired Staples, with his usual open and unabashed ignorance.

'Mr. Archibald St. Julian Staples,' said Rosemary, glancing up at him in half-impatient, half-disdainful disapprobation, ' *did* your parents send you to school ? '

' Yes ; there's been money enough spent on my education,' he replied.

'But not much to show for it,' retorted Rosemary, who, like Violet, had the habit of making Staples a butt for raillery, though in a less gentle and friendly tone. She had no patience with him, she was wont to say, whereas Violet manifested a great deal of that excellent virtue in his regard.

Not being ready at retort, Staples leant a stolid shoulder against the column of the piazza, looked straight before him, and puffed at his pipe not much more sulkily than usual.

Violet came to the rescue.

' Were you at college? ' she asked with mild interest.

'No. I was ploughed for smalls. Then I had another chance given me, and I failed for that too.'

'What a shame to put young men to such stiff examinations!' Violet observed sympathetically.

'It wasn't particularly stiff,' he replied candidly. 'I could have got through easily enough if I'd worked at all; but I never did work— never saw why I should. Always thought I was all right, till my old uncle went and married a young woman! If I'd known he was going to do such a thing, why, I suppose I should have read books like other fellows!'

'Don't you care at all for reading, then?'

'No; I don't care for anything—at least, I only like a few things. I like music, and horses, and dogs.'

'Miss Preston has seen you ride, and has

heard you swear,' remarked Tregelva ; ' but she hasn't heard you sing yet.'

' Do sing to us, Mr. Staples !' said Rosemary. 'I should like to hear you sing.'

' I sing in the small hours of the morning,' he replied seriously.

' Well, we could sit up, or rise early. I got up once to see the sunrise from the Rigi ; and I dare say it would be quite as well worth while.'

But Staples shook his head.

' I don't think you will hear me sing.'

The tropical twilight closes swiftly, like a curtain of shadow dropped upon the scene ; the golden clouds of sunset pale and die into misty greys and blues; and on the piazza, though the dark has fallen, the little group linger still, chatting, laughing, rallying each other, until a murmur of eager voices from within the house attracts their attention ; and, eager for the smallest diversion, they one and all hasten indoors and find in the central hall the two Fraser boys, Spencer, and Harrington, all grouped in a circle around young Chadwick, who stands under the lamp, with a smile of modest triumph on his boyish beardless face. He has a gun, as usual, in one hand. With the other he holds up, suspended by the wings, an unhappy owl—an enormous bird, which hangs flaccidly in his grasp. At the first glance the new arrivals can scarcely tell whether it is alive or dead, but are soon enlightened by the remarks of the surrounding group.

'Don't touch it. It'll bite.'

'They've awfully strong beaks.'

'It would eat a live mouse.'

'We haven't got a live mouse.' It is Conyers who offers this practical objection.

'It won't eat.'

'It won't live.'

'Put it in a cage.'

'Oh, poor thing! let it fly!' pleads Violet.

'It can't fly.   Its wing is broken.'

'And so is its leg.'

'Oh, d—— it, kill the poor brute!' says Staples with just a shade less indolent indifference than usual.

And after a variety of conflicting counsels and suggestions, it is his advice that is taken, it being decided by the majority of votes that the owl is too badly wounded to recover.

Young Chadwick, still cheerful and complacent—as willingly accepting the alternative of making a target for the second time of his unlucky captive, as that of keeping it in a cage and feeding it on live mice—bears his prey off into the garden, Harrington and Spencer following to witness the execution.

Staples steps aside to the smoking-room door and begins to fill his pipe, growling in an undertone :

'That fellow hasn't got any more feeling than a flea!'

Violet is standing near him; and they are sympathetically expressing congenial humanitarian sentiments on the subject of sport in general and the injured owl in particular, when two shots are heard in quick succession from the garden, and then an exclamation of—

'I declare! It's not dead yet!'

Staples turns abruptly, flings down his pipe and tobacco-pouch, with a string of expletives more or less unfit for ears polite, clears the whole flight of piazza-steps at a bound, and rushes across the lawn in the direction of the shots.

Violet runs out too, and follows him into the darkness of the moonless night, wherein she can just discern two or three black figures standing round a tree, and a shapeless fluttering something suspended from a branch.

Violet shudders a little as the figure she knows must be Staples seizes the dark fluttering thing, and she hears the sound of an almost human groan; then, a moment afterwards, Staples observes in calm and satisfied tones :

'That's done!'

'Oh, don't you feel rather like a murderer?' she asked.

'No, I feel as if I'd done one good thing to day,' he replied. 'It was a good deed to put that poor brute out of its pain.'

Then supper-time came, and Max Randolph, whom Mr. Whitworth had hospitably invited to drop in and sup; he rather liked Randolph, and, moreover, saw in him a possible purchaser —not in a large way of course; that could not be expected of a roving artist, but Mr. Whitworth had some choice small five acre groves on his list at modest prices eminently suitable for an artist's investment. And after supper they, as usual, sat out-of-doors a little while, Staples installing himself beside Violet, whilst Rosemary was a rose between two thorns, viz. Randolph and Conyers, and was perfectly well able to manage two thorns, three thorns, or even four thorns at once. Tregelva and Harrington were talking sport, and Chadwick relating the episode of the owl.

'Staples is a humanitarian,' remarked Tregelva. 'His language was choice when Chadwick shot the bird and didn't kill it.'

'You don't care for sport?' Violet observed to Staples.

'I like hunting big game,' he said. 'I'd like to hunt buffalo. I've been on an elephant-hunt in India. *That's* sport, when the elephant comes crashing through the wood, and you dodge and run for your life! But I don't see what you want to go and shoot poor little birds for. They're harmless little things; and they're pretty; and they sing. I like music. Won't you sing to us this evening?'

'Certainly—by-and-by.'

And by-and-by, when, one by one, they all had retreated from the falling night-dews and moved into the parlour, the piano was opened, and Staples lent his valuable assistance to Violet in looking over the music.

Staples might be, as he expressed himself, fond of music; but it was very evident that his education in that art had been neglected. He offered homage at a distance, and had never sought an intimate knowledge, or indeed any acquaintance at all with the muses.

'I'd like to learn the piano,' he observed, watching Violet's fingers run lightly over the keys. 'Are the black things sharps?'

'No,' she replied gravely, 'they are flats.'

'Where are the sharps, then?' he inquired; 'there are sharps in a piano, aren't there?'

'Yes, and elsewhere sometimes,' she remarked, 'but there isn't one very near here at present!'

'I suppose you mean you think I'm a flat, Miss Preston—is that it?'

'By no means,' she replied pleasantly. 'You're in my good books to-night, and I do not mean to say anything abusive.'

Staples smiled; he had one of those sweet smiles that often lighten up a somewhat sulky, heavy, downcast face. Violet had lately discovered that he had rather good eyes—large dog-like brown eyes—which now and then had something of the soft and dreamy wistfulness of an affectionate dog's upward look.

Musical evenings were now a regular institution at West Grove House; and the entertainment had developed in variety as, one by one, other performers had consented to be drafted into the programme. Harrington had a fairly good tenor voice; and the eldest Fraser could sing one song—at least he had never been known to sing any other; his one song was the 'Midshipmite.' Even Conyers had once been beguiled into uplifting a passable baritone voice in melody; but Staples could never be induced to do more than join in chorus. There were certain stock favourite songs which were always in demand. Rosemary was strong in songs of emotion and sentiment, and operatic airs, and her small but select audience were never tired of hearing the pathetic passion of her rich contralto thrilling in the 'Good-byes!' and 'For ever and for ever's,' of modern love-songs, while her dramatic rendering of the 'Habañera' air from 'Carmen' never failed to rouse a stir of something like enthusiasm in even this un-emotional audience.

Violet had struck out rather a specialty for herself in the line of the more pathetic of the negro melodies. She delighted everyone with the dear familiar old plantation song of the ' Suwanee River,' which, somehow, well-known as it is, yet never seems to become hackneyed. She distinguished herself in the pathos she lent to the quaintly characteristic ballad of ' Rosa Lee,' and always sang the solos in the equally characteristic negro hymns which were popular on Sunday evenings at the West Grove, the especial favourite being that one with a chorus of—

> Oh, dem golden slippers !
> Oh, dem golden slippers !
> Golden slippers we's gwine to wear
> To walk de golden street !

in which all the brotherhood would join in lustily, Lorenzo and Beverley generally listening in the hall delighted, and smiling from ear to ear. Although it takes a negro voice and accent to give the full aroma and flavour to these negro melodies, yet Violet had a certain soft and pathetic thrill in her voice which suited them—at least suited those which had a touch of pathos, and the purely comic ones she never sang.

This night Max Randolph, as usual, took up his position by the piano and turned over the leaves. He almost always did so ; it had become an institution that this should be his post. Conyers sat by the table in a statuesque but comfortable pose, with folded arms. Tregelva leant back in an arm-chair, languidly caressing his fair mustache. Staples, seeing Randolph in possession of the post he secretly coveted, but to which he had never yet attained, had cast himself limply, as if his joints all hung loose, on a sofa in a remote corner. Christie, tired out with a hard day's riding, stretched himself full length, with a frank word of apology, on the other sofa, accepted the musical performance of the evening as a serenade, and to all appearance availed himself of it as such.

Violet had been singing the 'Chanson de
Fortunio '—that most dainty and graceful of
love-songs ; and no voice was better fitted
to express its exquisite delicacy and tenderness than hers.

> ' Je fais ce que sa fantaisie
>    Veut m'ordonner,
> Et je veux, s'il lui faut ma vie,
>    La lui donner!
> Mais j'aime trop pour que je dis
>    Qui j'ose aimer,
> Et je veux mourir pour ma mie,
>    Sans la nommer ! '

Staples might have liked these words if he
had understood them, but in the present stage
of his education their simple charm was wasted
upon him.  He liked what he could compre-
hend, and so presently from his distant sofa
came a mournful entreaty—

'Please sing " Rosa Lee," Miss Preston.'

' Most musical, most melancholy,' Rosemary
commented on the lugubrious tone.  ' Really,

Mr. Staples, you ought to be a nightingale
yourself!

> It was the nightingale, and not the lark,
> That pierced the fearful hollow of mine ear.'

Violet was looking through a book of
ballads with Max Randolph, and, I fear, did not
bestow on Staples' pathetic appeal the attention
it deserved.

In a few minutes the despondent pleading
from the sofa was reiterated—

' I wish you *would* sing " Rosa Lee," Miss
Preston.'

Still Violet, absorbed with Max, was in-
attentive, until a third time a voice, that had
sunk to the deepest depths of dejection, be-
sought her—

' Oh, do sing " Rosa Lee," Miss Preston ! '

Then Violet at last put down the book of
ballads, and vouchsafed to treat him and the rest
of the company to the musical history of the love

and death of that black and beauteous Rose, whose 'Feet so large and comely too' seem to have been one of her chief charms in the eyes of her faithful 'foolish Joe.' Possibly with a view of atoning for her previous lack of attention, Violet now threw unusual pathos into the final lament—

U-la-ila ola-ee !
Rosa sleeps in Tennessee !

Staples was so well pleased that he got off the sofa and slouched across the room to the piano. As he neared that goal he suddenly remembered that his hands were buried deeply in his pockets, and plucked them forth with as much alacrity as was compatible with his general leisureness, not to say laziness, of move-ment.

Violet noted the action and appreciated it.

'Good boy !' she said with an approving

smile. ' I shall turn you out quite a reformed character yet ! '

' Why, Vi, do you think there's any room for improvement left ? ' exclaimed Rosemary.

' It's clear *you* do, Miss Heath,' with the faintest touch of resentment in his tone.

' I would fain be polite,' Rosemary replied, ' but stern conscience will *not* allow me to deny the charge. I think there *is* still a little room for—polish.'

Staples never entered into a war of words with Rosemary—perhaps because he was so well aware that he would get the worst of it. He kept close by Violet, and presently took advantage of Max Randolph's transference of attention to Rosemary to observe, with a sort of grievance in his air—

' I suppose I'll never get the chance of turning over your music for you. It's always Randolph.'

'You should turn over if you were near,' Violet replied amiably, 'but you never *are* near!'

'I will be next time, if you'll let me.'

But Violet would commit herself to no promise beyond

'First come, first served.'

END OF THE FIRST VOLUME.

www.ingramcontent.com/pod-product-compliance
Lightning Source LLC
Chambersburg PA
CBHW030818020726
47499CB00006B/1970